DEN

OF

THE

WHITE

FOX

DEN OF THE WHITE FOX

Lensey Namioka

Browndeer Press
Harcourt Brace & Company
San Diego   New York   London

Copyright © 1997 by Lensey Namioka

All rights reserved. No part of this publication may be reproduced or
transmitted in any form or by any means, electronic or mechanical, including
photocopy, recording, or any information storage and retrieval system,
without permission in writing from the publisher.

Requests for permission to make copies of any part of the work should
be mailed to: Permissions Department, Harcourt Brace & Company,
6277 Sea Harbor Drive, Orlando, Florida 32887-6777.

Browndeer Press is a registered trademark of Harcourt Brace & Company.

Library of Congress Cataloging-in-Publication Data
Namioka, Lensey.
Den of the White Fox/by Lensey Namioka.
p.   cm.
"Browndeer Press."
Summary: In medieval Japan, two out-of-work samurai warriors must use
their fighting skills when they join a group of local boys, led by the
mysterious White Fox, in resistance to a cruel occupying force.
ISBN 0-15-201282-6   ISBN 0-15-201283-4 pb
[1. Samurai—Fiction.   2. Japan—Fiction.]
I. Title.
PZ7.N1426De   1997
[Fic]—dc20   96-34840

Text set in Granjon
Designed by Ivan Holmes

First edition
F E D C B A
F E D C B A pb
Printed in Hong Kong

Characters

Zenta, a *ronin,* or masterless samurai
Matsuzo, a *ronin,* Zenta's pupil
Kinu, a young woman who lives in the valley
Jiro, her younger brother
Lord Yamazaki, a warlord who recently
    conquered the region
Gombei, a local man who enlisted in Lord
    Yamazaki's army
Tozaemon, Gombei's father
Busuke, local commander for Lord Yamazaki
Ballad singer
Shrine priest
Hachiro, a local teenage boy
Innkeeper
Serving maid at the inn
Tofu maker
Ito Tadayoshi, Lord Yamazaki's deputy
The White Fox

I

"By the time you reach the valley, the sun will be setting," said the girl. "It's an unwholesome place after dark."

She was standing at the front entrance of the inn, and she had greeted the two travelers with an invitation to stop at her establishment. Her warning about the valley could be just another ploy to gain customers, thought Matsuzo. Or perhaps not. The inn was a modest place, but it had a prosperous air. It didn't seem desperate for business.

The girl was very attractive and looked friendly. Matsuzo had the feeling that she was really concerned about their welfare, but maybe he was just flattering himself. That look of genuine concern was a valuable stock in trade for employees at an inn.

Aside from the attractiveness of the maid, however, Matsuzo was eager to stop for the day. He and Zenta had been walking since early morning, and the last climb up to the mountain pass had been steep. He was sticky with perspiration, for it was high summer. He was also grubby with dust from the road and more than ready for a bath.

"We're having fern tips for dinner tonight," added the girl. "And there's *ayu* caught from the stream just a few minutes ago. You can smell it grilling."

She was right. The smell of the charcoal-broiled fish reached Matsuzo's nose and started his mouth watering. He looked inquiringly at his companion. The two were in funds for once, and they had planned to take their ease until the money ran out.

The inn was set in a narrow mountain pass, and the prospect in front offered a striking view of misty hills and twisted pine trees. It promised tempting food and good service. What more could they possibly want? This seemed the ideal place for spending their time and their money.

Matsuzo was just about to speak when there was a shout from one of the back rooms of the inn. "The water's too hot! Where's that stupid maid?"

The girl looked behind her and cringed. "I'll be right back," she muttered.

"I don't want to stop here," Zenta said to Matsuzo, after the girl had run inside. "I'd rather go down to the valley this evening."

Matsuzo felt his temper rise—partly from irritation caused by the heat, and partly from exasperation. Zenta could be moody, and even when he had good reasons for his actions, he didn't always bother to explain them.

Matsuzo fought down his anger, however. Zenta was five years older, and was his chosen teacher. After a year of traveling together, Matsuzo had yet to meet anyone who surpassed Zenta in swordsmanship and the other martial arts.

Nevertheless, in some ways Matsuzo considered himself to be the more mature and more practical of the two. There had been occasions when Zenta gave way to whims that led them into difficulties, even danger. Matsuzo had to find out if this was one of Zenta's more reckless impulses. "All right. Tell me why you are so eager to visit this particular valley."

Zenta raised his basket hat to mop at his face. He looked faintly embarrassed. "I'm curious to investigate the place because I've heard people say it's haunted by the spirit of something called the White Fox."

When Matsuzo was a child, his nurse had told him stories about unlucky people who were tricked by a fox spirit. He'd enjoyed these stories, which were often funny, with the poor victim ending up robbed of both his money and his dignity by the fox. "You mean we're leaving this inn and going into the valley just because of some fairy tale?" he asked.

Before Zenta could answer, they heard the angry voice shouting again. It was joined by a second voice, even more overbearing. It was also very penetrating.

"Anyway, they seem to have some very demanding guests here already," said Zenta. "I don't want to share lodging with people like that."

Reluctantly, Matsuzo had to agree. The servants at the inn would be fully occupied satisfying the needs of the two loudmouthed guests. They would have little time for attending to anyone else. With another sigh, he turned and followed Zenta down the path that led to the valley.

After walking past the inn, the two men found the road descending steeply. It narrowed, forcing them to proceed in single file. In places they had to go down stone steps, and the drop was so sharp that they clutched at passing branches to steady themselves. Although the sun was not ready to set, the winding road was already getting dark. Visibility was further reduced by a mist, which thickened as they went.

It had been hot on the other side of the mountain pass, but as they descended, a cold fog soon wrapped itself around them. Matsuzo shivered, oppressed by the coolness and the quiet. "I'm beginning to see why the girl at the inn said it was unwholesome down here. It doesn't feel like summer at all. I hope we don't catch a chill."

"There *is* something unnatural about this place," said Zenta, as they continued their laborious descent into the valley. "I can't even hear insects! At this time of the year, you'd expect the cicadas to be loud and shrill."

Matsuzo was not interested in cicadas. He was longing for a soak in a fragrant cedar tub. After the bath, he looked forward to putting on a crisp, clean cotton kimono and sitting down to a meal served by a pretty girl, as pretty as the one they had just left at the inn.

The uncanny silence was broken by a sound —only it wasn't made by an insect. It was a dry, staccato bark.

The two men stopped and listened. But silence fell again. After a moment they began to walk on.

"Foxes make a kind of high barking sound," said Zenta.

"A white fox, no doubt," Matsuzo said dryly. But even as he said them, his words no longer sounded funny. It was all too easy to see the shapes of foxes in the swirling white mist around him.

The narrow mountain path was made treacherous by loose pebbles, and Matsuzo lost track of time as he struggled to place his feet. What made things worse was the thickening fog, which had become so dense that he could hardly see his hands in front of him. His clothes, damp with perspiration, stuck to his body in clammy swaths.

Concentrating on feeling the way with his feet, Matsuzo didn't know at first that he had fallen far behind his companion. Suddenly he realized that Zenta's footsteps were no longer audible.

He could see nothing; he could hear nothing. It was like being suspended alone in a huge void. He was overcome by panic. He had seen many Buddhist paintings of hell, full of sinners tormented by fire and hideous goblins. But hell must be more like this: just dead emptiness.

At least he still possessed his sense of smell. He could detect a faint but repulsive odor: the odor of something untamed.

Then Matsuzo heard the high, staccato bark again. There was no longer any possibility of a mistake: That bark told him the odor was the rank, feral smell of a fox. Very well, thought Matsuzo grimly. Zenta wanted to see foxes in this valley, and it seemed he would have his wish.

But where was Zenta? How long was it since he had last heard Zenta's steps? Matsuzo began to nurse a real grievance. He'd been deserted. Zenta had insisted on dragging him to this benighted valley, and now he had abandoned him and left him practically suspended in midair.

Muttering angrily, Matsuzo forced himself to trudge on. To his great relief, he found the narrow path flattening out, and he guessed that he was finally coming to the floor of the valley. The fog must have settled higher up in the hills, because he began to make out some shapes around him.

The path was not only flatter, but also wider. Soon he came to a clearing, and beyond that he saw a house. As the fog cleared, the outline of the house became sharper. It looked like a wretched hovel. Tall weeds grew on the sagging thatched roof. Up close, he could see holes in the mud-daubed walls through which the bamboo lattice showed.

Then his nose caught the scent of a charcoal fire. From behind the house appeared a wisp of smoke. Matsuzo's spirits lifted. The smoke must be coming from the charcoal fire he had smelled, and that meant a hot grill. *Something* had to be cooking there, even if it was only boiled millet.

He went cautiously up to the door of the hut, which was standing open. Just as he was about to call out a greeting, he stopped and stared.

Two people were seated on the wooden floor inside. One was a young woman. The other was Zenta. He was looking intently at the woman, and his stillness almost made him seem like someone spellbound.

For a wild moment, Matsuzo wondered if she could be a fox spirit who had assumed the form of a beautiful woman to entrap unwary travelers. That was a common theme in many of the fairy tales, and in most of them the traveler was lucky to escape with his life.

Matsuzo must have made some sound, for Zenta stirred and turned. "So there you are," he said to Matsuzo. "I wondered when you were going to catch up."

"You don't seem particularly worried," Matsuzo said dryly. Some of his anger returned. He took off his sandals, stepped up to the entrance, and greeted the young woman. "I'm Ishihara Matsuzo," he said stiffly. "Thank you for letting me intrude on you."

"Our hostess is Kinu," Zenta told Matsuzo. "Her family has lived in this valley for many generations. She is kind enough to offer us food and shelter."

The cramped, one-room house might be in miserable condition, but their hostess, Kinu, looked fresh and crisp in her clean cotton kimono. Typical of the kind worn by a countrywoman, it barely reached to her ankles, unlike the long, trailing kimono worn by high-ranking ladies. Her sash was secured with a careful knot, and her long hair was neatly tied back.

Up close, Matsuzo saw that she was striking rather than beautiful. Her face was thin and her features were strongly marked. Her figure was graceful and supple. In the diffused, misty light from the door, her skin had a sparkle, almost a glow.

She didn't seem at all cowed by the arrival of two armed samurai, and even Zenta appeared to be impressed by her self-assurance. He cleared his throat. "Now that there are two of us, we can't possibly impose on you. Surely there is an inn nearby, or some establishment that takes in paying guests?" He put a slight stress on the word *paying*.

The young woman smiled faintly at Zenta's attempt to be tactful. "Didn't they tell you, the people nearby, that we have very few visitors here? No inn could stay in business in the valley. Did you try the one up at the pass?"

"We thought about it," admitted Zenta. "But some guest with a very disagreeable voice was shouting inside, and we decided not to stay."

The young woman's smile broadened. "You must have heard Busuke. He commands Lord Yamazaki's occupation force here, and we know

9

his voice well. When he yells from the pass, I swear that we can hear him all the way down here."

"Occupation force?" asked Zenta. "Lord Yamazaki feels it necessary to station men in the valley?"

This time Kinu laughed. "Lord Yamazaki hasn't been in control of this region for very long. Perhaps he feels insecure about us."

She sounds actually proud that her people have succeeded in making Lord Yamazaki feel insecure, Matsuzo thought.

"How many of his men are stationed here?" asked Zenta.

"There are twenty in the valley, staying in some of the better houses," said the young woman. "Naturally, our house isn't good enough to accommodate any of the soldiers."

She seemed to be studying the two men. Matsuzo knew that for once they looked present-able. They were *ronin*, unemployed samurai, and they wandered around the country looking for work as mercenaries. There had been lean times when they looked hungry and desperate. But this time they had just come from an employer who had paid them well. They both wore neat kimonos and their hair had been combed, oiled, and tied in topknots. Matsuzo also knew that their speech, manners, and carriage should tell the woman that they were men of good family. They were not like the ruffians who plagued the country during these times of civil wars between rival warlords.

"You are quite welcome to stay in our house and share our humble dinner," Kinu said. Since Zenta had not mentioned her surname, she was not a member of the samurai class. Nevertheless her manner was not at all humble—even if her dinner was.

Zenta made one more effort. "We are *ronin* and therefore unemployed, but we do have ample money. Please accept something, at least for purchasing foodstuff, so that we won't be a burden on you."

"Money won't do much good," said Kinu. "There are only two shops selling food here: the dumpling shop and the tofu maker's. They're probably both closed by now."

Matsuzo joined Zenta on the floor. He had to avoid places where the floorboards were split. Kinu had not mentioned a husband or a father. Before Matsuzo could ask her whether there was anyone else in the household, Kinu excused herself and told them that she had to attend to her charcoal brazier in back of the house.

The two men examined the one-room interior of the cottage. A sunken fireplace occupied the middle of the room, but since it was summer, the ashes were cold and the cooking was being done outdoors. The wooden floor was scrupulously polished, and the straw pads they were sitting on were clean, though worn.

Some sliding doors on one side of the room must contain cupboards for the folded bedding. Would there be enough futons for the guests? wondered Matsuzo. Even if there were, they would most likely be as thin as rice crackers. From what he had seen of Kinu's management, however, he guessed that the bedding would at least be very clean.

Quick, light footsteps sounded outside, and the two samurai instantly reached for their swords. They put them down again when they heard a young voice calling, "I'm home!"

A boy bounded into the room, and at the sight of two strangers, he stopped dead. He was holding a packet wrapped in bamboo leaf, which he suddenly clutched tightly to his chest.

Kinu appeared in the doorway. "Oh, so you're back, finally. What's that you're holding?"

"Somebody gave these to me," the boy said simply. He held out the packet.

Instead of taking it, Kinu said, "Where are your manners? Greet our guests!"

The boy turned red. He stooped down to the floor and bowed, murmuring an unintelligible greeting.

Kinu grimaced. "This graceless boy is my younger brother, Jiro," she told the two *ronin*. "You'll have to put up with him, I'm afraid, since he is the only male in the household. Our parents are dead, and the two of us live alone here."

Jiro got up from his bow. The resemblance between brother and sister was strong. The boy also had sharply marked features, and moved with the same grace and suppleness. His rounder cheeks, however, made him seem softer.

The boy shared Kinu's rather unusual self-assurance, Matsuzo noted. He might take orders from his sister, but he didn't seem overawed by the presence of the two samurai. The glance he gave them had a touch of impudence. Give him a few years, thought Matsuzo, and the boy will no doubt become as sardonic as Kinu.

Again Jiro held out the packet, and this time Kinu took it and unwrapped the bamboo leaf. "Rice dumplings!" she exclaimed. She stared at her brother. "Where did you get them? You know we can't afford these!"

Matsuzo looked wistfully at the packet. He was getting very hungry.

"I told you . . ." Jiro began.

Before he could say any more, a sharp rap sounded on the door.

"You won't escape again!" said a deep voice.

"We saw you running home, and we've caught you with the stolen goods this time!"

A tall, burly figure pushed into the room. Behind him was another man, slimmer in build. The first man paused when he saw the two *ronin*. "Who are you?" he demanded.

"We are guests of this household," Zenta replied calmly. "We've been invited to stay." He stressed the word *invited*.

The first man snorted. "Don't be insolent! We're in charge of order in this valley, and we don't allow thieves to run loose!"

"Are you suggesting that we are thieves?" Zenta asked gently. His voice was soft, but there was something in it that made the intruder draw back.

The second man stepped around his companion and entered the room. There was a gasp from Kinu when she saw him. "Gombei!" she exclaimed. "Would you please explain the meaning of this intrusion?"

The man called Gombei had pleasant, regular features, except for his mouth, which was oddly twisted. Matsuzo wondered if Gombei suffered from some affliction. Then he realized that the man was acutely embarrassed.

"We have to investigate, Kinu," muttered Gombei, avoiding her gaze. "We can't let these thefts continue."

"What thefts?" demanded Kinu. She was staring at him with glittering eyes. Even the first man, the aggressive one, seemed abashed and retreated to the door. Matsuzo guessed that there was some past history between Kinu and Gombei.

Gombei took a deep breath. "Your brother was seen running away with stolen food, Kinu. I'm very sorry, but we have orders to take him into custody."

"And of course you volunteered eagerly for this duty," Kinu said bitterly.

"I volunteered because I can make sure that Jiro isn't treated roughly," protested Gombei.

Kinu's face was very pale. "You're making a mistake, Gombei."

"There's no mistake," said the first man. "We've had so many thefts recently that we set up a special team of watchers. The dumpling shop was one of the places we were watching. Your brother was definitely seen in the neighborhood when the theft was discovered."

Jiro opened his mouth, but Zenta spoke first. "Are you talking about these dumplings here? We bought these for Kinu at that inn on top of the hill."

"You're lying!" snarled the first officer.

"Now, why would I want to do that?" Zenta asked with wide eyes.

There was a long pause. Gombei's mouth

twisted again. Pulling his companion back, he said, "There's nothing more we can do here. Let's go."

At the door he looked back. "Kinu, tell your brother to be more careful in the future about choosing his friends."

2

After the two officers left, Matsuzo said jokingly, "I hope he wasn't referring to us."

Nobody smiled. Kinu asked Zenta, "Why did you lie about the dumplings?"

"I lied because your brother Jiro did not lie," replied Zenta. "I believe he told the truth when he said somebody gave the packet to him."

"Jiro," Kinu said, staring earnestly at her brother, "who gave these dumplings to you?"

Jiro looked away. "I promised not to tell."

The boy really *should* be more careful about choosing his associates, thought Matsuzo. "Your so-called friend," he said, "may have passed these stolen dumplings on to you when he saw those officers on his trail."

Jiro was on the verge of tears. He was about thirteen years old, but at the moment he seemed much younger.

"Wash your hands, Jiro, and get ready to eat supper," Kinu said, sighing with exasperation.

She grinned suddenly, and for a moment she looked younger and her features seemed softer. "We may as well enjoy the dumplings these gentlemen have been generous enough to buy for us."

Even with the addition of the dumplings, supper was not lavish. When interrupted by the arrival of the two *ronin,* Kinu had apparently been boiling some burdock roots. Matsuzo liked these roots well enough cooked with other things, but by themselves they were too earthy for his taste. Kinu had also made miso soup. Containing only a small amount of the precious bean paste, the soup was thin, almost transparent. The dumplings were therefore highly welcome. Matsuzo was too hungry and too polite to complain about the absence of condiments like pickled ginger.

Since the meal was simple, Kinu did not have to spend much time clearing away and washing the dishes. Afterward she slid open the cupboards and began to take out bedding.

Matsuzo glanced at Jiro, who was idly picking at the ashes in the fireplace with a pair of iron chopsticks. "What was the officer talking about?" he asked the boy. "Has there been a lot of theft here in the valley?"

Jiro stuck the chopsticks back in the ash and dusted his hands. "Most of the people here are hungry. But I've noted that those who cooperate with our new overlords have more food than they need." Matsuzo could hear the bitterness in the boy's voice.

Kinu, who had been spreading the futon out on the floor, said over her shoulder, "I can understand starving children snatching some food. But clothes and even money have been stolen as well."

Zenta finished polishing his swords with a square of silk cloth. He folded away the cloth and looked up at his hostess. "The items were stolen from those who had cooperated with the new overlords, I presume? Perhaps the thieves were simply expressing their resentment."

Kinu shook out a quilt with a sharp snap. "Some people are simply thieves because they like to steal! Then they try to justify the theft by claiming some lofty motive."

"They're telling Lord Yamazaki's soldiers that they won't tolerate oppression here," declared Jiro.

" 'Tolerate oppression'! Where did you learn a pretentious phrase like that?" demanded Kinu. She lifted her head proudly. "The people of this valley do not resort to theft, whatever the reason."

"You people here have illustrious ancestors," murmured Zenta. "You're descended from the Heike, aren't you?"

So that was it! The two of them weren't visiting the valley only because of the White Fox, thought Matsuzo. Zenta must have heard something about the inhabitants here. No wonder Kinu carried herself so proudly, if she counted the Heike as her ancestors.

Everyone knew that four hundred years ago, the Heike clan had been the most powerful one in the country. Leaders of the clan even married their daughters into the imperial family. But war broke out between the Heike and their rivals, the Genji clan. Many ballads had been written about battles between the two, which ended when the Heike were defeated and almost completely annihilated. A few surviving family members and their supporters had managed to escape, however, and there were rumors that their descendants lived in various isolated valleys, such as this one.

Matsuzo glanced at Kinu and Jiro with more interest: They may have become peasants, and their valley occupied by a neighboring warlord, but they hadn't forgotten their proud history.

Kinu's face softened, and for a moment she looked almost beautiful. She smiled with genuine warmth at Zenta. "Ah, so you've heard about us. Now you see why we couldn't possibly stoop to thievery."

"And it's why I believed your brother when he said he didn't take the dumplings," said Zenta, smiling back.

There is still the question of who *did* steal the

dumplings, thought Matsuzo. Zenta did not ask that question. Instead, he said to Jiro, "Tell me about the foxes that are supposed to haunt this valley."

Jiro didn't answer. Instead he picked up the iron chopsticks again and began poking furiously at the fireplace ash. Before Zenta could repeat the question, Kinu frowned at Jiro. "Stop making a mess with those ashes! Anyway, it's almost time for bed."

Matsuzo wondered if a thirteen-year-old boy, and the only male in the family, would submit to orders from a sister. Jiro glowered for a moment at Kinu. Then he sighed theatrically and rolled his eyes at the two guests. In the end, however, he put down the chopsticks and obeyed.

Kinu turned back to Zenta. "There isn't much to tell about the foxes," she said shortly. "We have a shrine in the valley dedicated to Inari, the grain deity. As you know, foxes are always associated with Inari."

Jiro, who had been getting ready for bed, stopped and slowly turned around. "People here are saying that the thefts are committed by the White Fox," he said quietly.

"Then tell me about the White Fox," said Zenta. "Is he some local supernatural spirit?"

Kinu shook her head impatiently. "It's just a story the children made up. Nobody believes it."

"My friends believe it!" said Jiro. He had unfolded and spread out his futon, but he showed no sign of going to bed.

"The same friends who gave you the package of dumplings?" asked Matsuzo.

Jiro turned away and crawled under the covers. "People who make fun of the White Fox always regret it afterward!"

Zenta cleared his throat. "On our way down into the valley, we did hear a kind of high bark. It sounded a bit like a fox."

For a moment nobody spoke. The only sound in the room was the clatter of Kinu putting away the supper dishes. Then she turned to Zenta. Her eyes were cold. "What's surprising about that? There are plenty of wild animals here in the valley: monkeys, boars—of course there would be foxes."

A *humph* came from under Jiro's covers. Matsuzo felt satisfied with Kinu's explanation. It had to be true.

Zenta was less easily satisfied, apparently. "Is there a legend specifically connected with foxes that are white?" he asked.

Kinu didn't reply at once. Finally she nodded. "There is some such story—not surprising when we've got an Inari shrine. But as far as I know, the White Fox of the legend has never been known to steal. If you really want to know more about it, you should ask our ballad singer. He knows all these tales."

Her lips tightened when she finished speaking, and there seemed little hope that she would tell them more.

Matsuzo yawned. He'd lost interest. It had been a long day, and he was ready for bed. But first he wanted to wash off the travel dust. It was unlikely that there would be a bathhouse at Kinu's humble home.

"Where do the people bathe around here?" he asked. "Is there a natural spring nearby?"

Kinu nodded. "There is a hot spring just down the road. The locals like it because the water has minerals good for various aches and pains. At this time of the night it won't be crowded."

The two men rose. "In that case, we'll visit the bath before retiring," said Zenta. "We'll try not to disturb you when we come back."

The sun had set. The moon was up and it was half full, but its light was dimmed by the fog, which had finally descended into the valley, and the two men had to make their way carefully along the path. Fortunately, the pool Kinu had mentioned was not far away. Soon they were following their noses, for they could smell the slightly sulfurous water. They found the small pool only a step away from the path. Steam rose from it and merged with the fog. The water

23

looked so inviting that the two men lost no time in getting undressed.

As Matsuzo folded his kimono, he noticed that Zenta was tying his swords and his clothes together with his sash and fastening them to a tree. "So you believe what Gombei said about thefts?" he asked.

"There's no point in taking a chance," said Zenta. He walked over to the pool and gently lowered himself into the water. "Ah . . . the temperature is just right!"

Matsuzo thought Zenta was being overcautious, but he decided to follow his friend's example, although he felt foolish as he tightened the knot of his sash around his bundle of clothes.

Zenta was right about the temperature of the water. It was perfect: hot enough to make them perspire freely, but not hot enough to cause real agony. The sulfurous water smelled of rotten eggs, a sign that it was effective in curing people of their aches.

Balancing his hand towel on his head, Matsuzo lowered himself down until the water almost covered his chin. He closed his eyes in bliss. "I hope we don't get attacked by monkeys, boars, foxes, or other wildlife here," he murmured. He was speaking partly to reassure himself. Isolated by the fog around them, he again had the feeling that outside of their immediate vicinity nothing existed, only a vast void.

He felt a nudge.

"Did you hear that?" whispered Zenta.

Raising himself up until his shoulder was out of the water, Matsuzo listened intently. His ears caught the sound of a sharp bark, similar to the one they had heard earlier. This was followed by a rustle behind him.

Matsuzo whirled around to see what was at his back. He was too slow and almost missed seeing the person in white—*the thing*—that was emerging out of the mist. It had human hands, he was almost sure, but it had the head of a fox. The wide mouth curved in a cruel grin and the chin came to a sharp point. The eyes were those of a wild animal.

Before Matsuzo could say anything, a huge wave washed over his face. Blinking to clear his eyes, he realized that the splash had been caused by Zenta leaping out of the pool.

"I've lost him!" said Zenta's voice.

"What was it?" sputtered Matsuzo. He wiped his face with his towel and tried to climb up the muddy side of the pool. But his arms and legs were trembling, and he slipped back once before he managed to scramble out.

"Somebody grabbed at my clothes," Zenta

said grimly. "It was a good thing I fastened them to the tree."

Matsuzo took a few deep breaths and tried to steady his racing heart. "You were right after all," he said finally. "If we hadn't tied our things to the tree, they'd be gone by now."

It was hopeless to chase after the thief—the fox—whatever it was. Because of the fog they couldn't see more than five paces in front of them.

Suddenly, Matsuzo could hear chuckles and muffled laughter all around them. Again he had that suffocating sense of isolation. There could be dozens or even hundreds of people around them, and he could see none of them!

Despite the summer heat and the hot soak, he turned cold. To stop his shivering he rubbed himself briskly with his towel, and he gritted his teeth to prevent them from chattering. He refused to be intimidated. He and Zenta were together this time. They might be surrounded, but they were not helpless. He saw that Zenta had already begun to dress himself.

As Matsuzo bent down for his clothes, a sudden thought struck him. "At least this will settle the question of whether Jiro belongs to this gang of mischief makers. Kinu can tell us if her brother left the house tonight—unless they're in it together."

Zenta shook his head. "I don't believe for a

moment that Jiro or his sister is working with the thief who took the dumplings and tried to steal our clothes just now. I'm looking forward to meeting that ballad singer Kinu mentioned. He might be able to tell us about the thefts and the White Fox."

Matsuzo nodded. "That bark we heard just now certainly sounded like a fox."

Walking back to Kinu's house, they did not hear any more of the mocking laughter. They found the house quiet except for Jiro's regular breathing. He presented a convincing picture of a tired boy sleeping deeply.

Kinu, not yet in bed, sat sewing by the light of a small oil lamp. She looked quiet and composed, not like someone who had been running recently. She looked up as they entered. Her eyes, larger than average, slanted up at the corners and had a reddish tint in the lamplight.

"You didn't have to waste lamp oil and wait up for us," Zenta said to their hostess. "We can see our way around in here."

"I have some darning to do, anyway," said Kinu. She turned back to her sewing. "Jiro's clothes have a way of falling apart on him. I think his bones must stick out and poke holes in the cloth."

She tried to smile, to show that she had spoken in jest. But Matsuzo guessed how much it cost her proud spirit to admit that her brother was undernourished and his clothes were literally in rags.

"He's not that bony," Zenta said gently. "Although it's true that he doesn't have much spare fat on him. Things must be hard, with only the two of you. Don't you have any other family?"

"My mother and my elder brother, Taro, died five years ago from a fever epidemic that swept through our valley." Kinu's voice became husky. She swallowed. "Then my father died last year." She wasn't quite successful in hiding the fact that she missed her parents and elder brother greatly.

Matsuzo looked around at the shabby room. Even when alive, Kinu's parents probably hadn't had much money to spare. "Your family grew mostly rice? The land here is uneven and rocky. You must find it hard to maintain the terracing for the rice paddies."

Kinu bent down again to her sewing. "My father earned some additional income . . . teaching."

I wonder what he taught, thought Matsuzo.

"Anyway, Jiro is growing fast, and soon he will be able to help me with the rice paddies," Kinu said shortly, refusing pity. She looked up. "You didn't spend much time at the pool."

"Somebody tried to steal our things," said Matsuzo. "But he didn't get them." After a moment, he added, "We heard a barking sound, like that of a fox. There was also some laughter."

Kinu looked at him for a moment, but said nothing as she began to put her sewing away. She folded Jiro's kimono and smoothed the cloth tenderly.

"Foxes are territorial," said Zenta, after a pause.

Why did he seem unable to abandon the subject of foxes? Matsuzo wondered.

"Perhaps the White Fox thinks we are intruding on his domain. He and his followers might be trying to drive us out," Zenta said.

Startled, Matsuzo glanced at Zenta. He talks about the White Fox as if he actually accepts its existence!

"You can't believe everything you hear," said Kinu. She didn't explain whether she was talking about the legend of the White Fox or the barks they had heard. She turned away, making it clear that the discussion was at an end.

Zenta sat down and arranged his swords next to him. Kinu had already spread out the futons and quilts for her guests. Matsuzo felt himself being overcome by fatigue, and wasted no time crawling under the covers.

Despite his fatigue he couldn't sleep at first. He could hear the soft voices of Zenta and Kinu discussing the recent occupation of the valley by

Lord Yamazaki's men. It disturbed Matsuzo that Zenta seemed to value Kinu's opinion and treat her with such deference.

Matsuzo respected Zenta for his judgment, his skill in arms, and his coolness in the face of danger. But Zenta had lost his parents and had left home at the age of fifteen. He had little experience of home life or knowledge of the ways of women. Matsuzo recalled instances when Zenta had admired women who had turned out to be completely ruthless. Kinu could be one of these. Matsuzo found her too controlled for his own taste. He liked women who were warmer and more impulsive.

So Zenta had decided to come to this strange, uncomfortable valley simply on a whim, because he wanted to investigate white foxes—or worse, to visit this proud descendant of the Heike.

Why would Zenta, who was anything but stupid or childish, be so fascinated by a tale of a white fox, the stuff of bedtime stories? It almost seemed as if Zenta were compelled to prove personally that every legend had a rational explanation.

On more than one occasion, the two of them had gone out of their way to investigate some rumor of the supernatural. Matsuzo shuddered as he remembered his harrowing experiences in a village haunted by a vampire cat. Nor could he forget their visit to an island overrun by flesh-eating ogres. The so-called ogres had turned out to be human, of course, but the two of them had barely escaped with their lives.

As Matsuzo began to fall asleep, it occurred to him that he and Zenta would be free to leave as soon as they succeeded in showing that the White Fox was only a human being or the product of local superstition. It would be an easy task that shouldn't take them long.

3

When Matsuzo opened his eyes and sat up, he discovered that he was the last one to awaken. All the other futons in the room had been folded and put away, and his was the only one still spread out on the floor. There was enough daylight to tell him that the morning was well advanced.

He had slept more soundly than he had intended. The hard walking and the heat must have exhausted him. He yawned, then got up quickly, straightened his kimono, and retied his sash. Feeling a little embarrassed at oversleeping, he stepped to the door and looked out.

The mist had cleared, and for the first time he could see the valley clearly. He stepped down and looked around. Kinu's house was more dilapidated than he had realized. But this morning the tan-colored mud walls had a cheerful golden glow from the sun, and delicate white flowers were growing among the weeds on the roof.

Around a corner he found Zenta and Jiro talking together. Both of them had their sleeves tied up with cords, as if they were about to fight. Fight? Why would an experienced warrior like Zenta fight with a thirteen-year-old boy?

Jiro raised a hand and beckoned to Zenta, who advanced slowly and suddenly made a rush at the boy. What happened next was over so quickly that Matsuzo wasn't sure what he had really seen.

Jiro seemed to give way under the attack, and Zenta made a complete somersault, bounced up on his feet, and spun around to stare at the boy. Matsuzo, who knew Zenta well, could tell that the somersault had been unintentional.

Both combatants stood and looked at each other. As if at a signal, they simultaneously dropped their hands and sighed.

"Wherever did you learn to do that?" asked Zenta. He sounded almost breathless, but it was probably from surprise.

Jiro grinned ruefully. "You're supposed to be flat on your back. I need more practice, obviously. It's something my friends and I have been... ah... taught. Jujitsu, it's called."

"Jujitsu," murmured Zenta slowly. "Yes, I think I've heard the term. *Jitsu* is skill and *ju* is softness, so *jujitsu* is a technique using the

33

principle of softness. You didn't use any opposing force. You just let me rush forward, and then directed my own momentum against me."

Matsuzo approached. "Who's been teaching you?" he asked Jiro. He had vaguely heard of the technique, and knew it had been developed some forty years earlier by Takenouchi Hisamori, who had borrowed from various sources: traditional wrestling, even fighting techniques from the Ryukyu Islands.

"I can't tell you," muttered Jiro, turning away. "We practice in secret, since we don't want the soldiers to know about it."

"Well, it's undignified," said Matsuzo primly. "A samurai shouldn't have to descend to this sort of thing."

"You say that because you samurai can carry swords," retorted Jiro. "We can't, so we have to learn empty-hand techniques, like jujitsu."

Jiro was obviously proud that his fighting technique could challenge a samurai. Suddenly his smile faded. Matsuzo turned around and saw that Kinu had appeared silently and was watching them. She was frowning. Jiro, who had been confident and even cocky a moment ago, now looked down and shuffled his feet.

"Is this how you keep your secrets?" Kinu asked her brother. Looking at her stony face,

Matsuzo decided that she was a bad person to cross.

"It's my fault, I'm afraid," Zenta said to her. "I asked Jiro how he and his friends amused themselves, and he mentioned that they practiced some martial exercises. So of course I became curious and asked for a demonstration."

"That's no excuse," said Kinu coldly. She didn't say whether it was Jiro or Zenta who was not excused.

Zenta lowered his eyes. For a moment it looked as if he might even shuffle his feet like Jiro. Matsuzo had never seen his friend being scolded before, and discovered that he rather enjoyed being a witness.

After a strained pause, Kinu turned to the house. "Breakfast is ready, such as it is," she said curtly.

Breakfast consisted of barley gruel without any white rice. Some pickled wild vegetables served as a side dish for the gruel. Looking at the simple meal, Matsuzo felt guilty. At this rate, the two of them would be consuming the last of Kinu's scanty supplies. She was too proud to accept money, so he and Zenta would have to think of some other way to repay her.

It didn't take long to finish the meager breakfast. Clearing away the dishes, Kinu looked at her brother. "I don't want you showing off your ju-jitsu to our guests again. They were too polite to laugh at you, but you're trying their patience."

"On the contrary," Zenta told Kinu sincerely, "I was very impressed. If I hadn't known that he was going to try something tricky, I would have been thrown to the ground." It was clear that he was eager to find out more about how the valley people came to practice jujitsu.

"The boy likes to play at fighting," Kinu said shortly. "Thank you for humoring him." It was equally clear that she had no intention of satisfying Zenta's curiosity.

"It was more than play," Zenta persisted. "For someone small and not particularly husky, that was the most effective way of fighting."

"We have to use the principle of *ju* here in the valley," Jiro said quickly. "That's how we manage to endure centuries of occupation by others."

He sounds like someone repeating a lesson, thought Matsuzo. He wondered whose it was. Then it occurred to him that even a woman could use the fighting technique, especially someone lithe and supple like Kinu.

"Jujitsu is certainly useful when you are un-armed," Zenta said thoughtfully.

"We're not allowed to carry any weapons here," Jiro said bitterly. "My friend, Hachiro, made a small bow and arrow out of some branches. He was only going to shoot the birds eating up his mother's rice field. But one of the soldiers grabbed the bow and gave Hachiro a terrible beating. They're all bullies. Busuke, their commander, is the worst. He actually enjoys hurting people."

Since Lord Yamazaki's men are ruling over people seething with resentment, thought Matsuzo, it isn't surprising that the locals are banned from carrying weapons. A bow, even a small one handled by a boy, could inflict serious damage.

"How many of you practice this jujitsu method?" Zenta asked Jiro. "Do you have a teacher?"

"That's enough of that!" snapped Kinu. "Jiro, instead of getting in my way here, why don't you make yourself useful? Take our guests to the ballad singer. He can tell them about the legend of the White Fox."

Jiro got up promptly. Matsuzo was also ready to leave. The last thing he wanted was to get in Kinu's way. His hostess could be daunting, and he began to see why Jiro, and even Zenta, looked cowed.

Led by Jiro, the two *ronin* set out on the same path they had taken before. They went past the pool where they had bathed the previous night. Soon they saw a number of village houses, some even more dilapidated than Jiro's.

Then the road widened and the dwellings became more spacious. A few even had bamboo fences around them, with gates. Jiro's lip curled as he walked by. "Some of Lord Yamazaki's soldiers are staying with those families over there," he said scornfully.

The houses accommodating the soldiers were in decidedly better condition than Jiro's. It obviously paid to collaborate with the conquerors.

"Even these houses aren't good enough for Busuke, the commander," sneered Jiro. "So he and one of his men are staying at the inn up at the pass."

Zenta nodded and Matsuzo remembered the loud, hectoring voice he had heard at the inn. That must have been the commander or one of his men. But Matsuzo said nothing. He didn't want to get involved with the problems of Lord Yamazaki's occupation. All over the country, territory was constantly changing hands as rival warlords fought to increase their domains. It was no business of theirs.

It was early morning, and the heat had not yet reached the valley floor. Shaded by trees on either side, the path they took was pleasantly cool. It followed a stream, and soon brought them to a small mill with a water wheel.

"They grind soybeans there to make tofu," said Jiro. He tried to sound indifferent, but he couldn't quite hide the longing in his voice. The food Kinu served wouldn't satisfy the appetite of a growing boy, Matsuzo thought, and tofu must seem like a treat to Jiro.

The road began to climb, and the trees on either side grew thick. Soon they found themselves in a clearing, and in front of them was a *torii,* the vermilion-colored wooden gate of a Shinto shrine. A thick rope hung with folded white paper streamers dangled from the gate.

Inari was the deity associated with rice and other grains. Since the majority of people's livelihood depended on agriculture, these shrines were common up and down the country. Foxes were said to be messengers of the deity, and therefore Inari shrines were always decorated with statues of foxes carved from stone.

This Inari shrine was no exception. As Jiro led the two samurai through the *torii* gate, they saw a pair of stone foxes standing guard on either side of the path. The stone was granite, but so finely textured that in the morning light it gleamed like white porcelain. As usual, the fox on the right had one front paw raised. The tip of the paw had been broken off.

Matsuzo saw that the break was fresh. Jiro followed his glance. "Another act by our friendly occupation force," he growled. He walked on, but there was no mistaking his outrage.

"Is this where we can expect to find the ballad singer?" Zenta asked Jiro.

The boy nodded. "He doesn't have a real home, and he spends a lot of time at the inn up in the pass. But he's also good friends with the shrine priest, so we're likely to find him here."

Jiro was right. They could hear the sounds of the *biwa,* or four-stringed lute, as they walked up the stone path leading to the main hall of the shrine.

Turning a corner, they came to a pavilion with a thatched roof. The eaves of the pavilion were hung with *ema,* pictures painted on wooden boards, mostly of horses. The pictures were offerings to Inari from worshipers grateful for a good harvest. To Matsuzo, the paintings looked crude, probably the work of local artists. A few of them had been hacked about. Art critics, perhaps?

Seated on the steps of the pavilion were three figures. One was the officer called Gombei, who had come to Kinu's house the previous night. The second man at the pavilion wore a small black cap tied under the chin, which identified him as the shrine priest. The third man was the lute player. Accompanying himself on the instrument, the ballad singer was describing the former glories of the Heike family.

Jiro stopped and listened enrapt to the story of

his ancestors. Even Matsuzo found the recital deeply moving, heard in this setting and in this company.

Suddenly the ballad singer stopped. The silence seemed almost harsh. Then he called out, "Who is there?"

His hearing was acute, of course. Like almost all ballad singers, he was blind, and his hearing had developed to make up for his lost sight.

"It's Jiro," announced the boy. "I've brought two visitors to meet you. They're staying with us, and they want to hear about the White Fox."

The two samurai walked up to the pavilion and introduced themselves. The shrine priest greeted them and welcomed them to the precincts. He had eyebrows so thick and active that they seemed to have an independent life of their own. Something in his bearing hinted at a military career before entering the priesthood, Matsuzo noted. He might be the priest of a shrine in a remote valley, but he didn't look like someone who had retired from active life. "The White Fox?" he exclaimed, and laughed, his eyebrows jiggling.

The other two men in the pavilion laughed as well. For some reason, they found the mention of the White Fox amusing. Today the officer, Gombei, looked more relaxed. Smiling, he said, "I should like to hear the story of the White Fox again, too. That rascal is being blamed for the wave of thefts in our region."

"Very well," said the ballad singer. "I yield to popular demand." He had a thin, sensitive-looking face. Even when he wasn't laughing, his expression contained a quality of joyous mirth that was infectious.

Plucking a lilting tune on his lute, the singer began to declaim with an exaggerated, dramatic delivery.

In the beginning, Inari found this valley
auspicious. To attend the deity came foxes.
A shrine was erected in honor of Inari, and
in its precincts are foxes held sacred.

Then the sound of the lute became darker, and the singer's voice lost its mock heroic tone.

Strangers came to our valley and oppressed
our people. They dared to show disrespect
to our shrine! They marred our offerings to
the deity and mutilated the statue of our
fox.

So the broken paw and the hacked pictures had been deliberate acts of vandalism, Matsuzo thought. Whoever was guilty of this desecration could certainly provoke the anger of the offended deity. The singer went on:

The White Fox, the guardian spirit of all the shrine foxes, cannot ignore this insult. It will punish the oppressors! It will drive them from our valley.

The singer stopped. In the sudden silence, someone drew a sharp breath. Matsuzo looked around quickly. That line about driving the oppressors from the valley had elicited a strong reaction from someone. Was it Jiro? Or was it Gombei, who was part of the occupation force?

The singer grinned at his audience. "Of course I don't believe a word of it," he said in a normal speaking voice.

"But . . . but . . ." began Jiro.

"So you *don't* think the White Fox is really the guardian spirit and protector of the shrine?" asked Zenta.

"Of course not," said the singer, turning in his direction. "The White Fox has a frivolous nature. Guarding the shrine is full-time work, and the White Fox would get bored."

"You seem to understand how the mind of the White Fox works," remarked Zenta.

"It takes one frivolous mind to understand another," the ballad singer replied lightly.

Jiro obviously wanted to protest, but he kept silent. The priest was smiling and his eyebrows danced up and down. There was an angry spark in his eyes, however.

Gombei's face was again screwed in a grimace. This time Matsuzo thought that the officer looked not so much embarrassed as resentful. He wondered whom Gombei resented.

Zenta broke the silence. "Your story tells about interlopers who came into the valley and offended the spirit of the Inari shrine," he said to the singer. "I wonder if by interlopers you mean the Heike, who came here after their defeat?"

"Of course not!" said the priest, looking shocked. He no longer tried to hide his displeasure. "The Heike have been here for centuries! The interlopers are the soldiers of Lord Yamazaki, who have made themselves obnoxious to everyone." He glanced briefly at Gombei. "Or to almost everyone."

Gombei flushed. "By being obnoxious, you mean arresting a thief who thought he could steal with impunity?" He turned to Zenta. "I come from this valley, and I count the Heike as my ancestors. However, I left several years ago and enlisted in the army of Lord Yamazaki." His lips twisted bitterly. "When Lord Yamazaki's forces came to occupy this valley, some of the people here began calling me a traitor."

"These days territory changes hands constantly and alliances shift," Zenta said calmly. "It's hard to say who is a traitor and who is not."

Zenta and Matsuzo had no right to criticize Gombei for enlisting with Lord Yamazaki, especially since he had done so before the warlord had invaded the valley.

"But tell me," Zenta asked Gombei, "what do *you* think about the White Fox? Do you think he's human, just a common thief, and not a supernatural spirit at all?"

Again Zenta is harping on the supernatural! Matsuzo thought. For himself, Matsuzo was ready to accept the idea that their mockers at the bathing pool were simply thieves and malicious troublemakers.

Gombei, however, frowned at Zenta's question. "When I was a child my mother used to tell me stories about the White Fox. He was no ordinary thief."

The singer scraped his fingers rapidly over the strings of his lute. The sound was somehow rude. "So when your friend lost his dagger, or when the rice shop owner had a packet of dumplings snatched from under his nose, it was just the work of some mischievous child! That must be why you are arresting little boys like Jiro."

Jiro blushed and looked down in confusion. Gombei's face turned a darker and angrier red. "I did not arrest Jiro," he said between his teeth. "I only visited his home last night to deliver a timely warning. If Busuke had gone instead, Jiro would not be standing here with a whole skin!"

"Have it your way," the ballad singer said lightly. "The day is too hot for quarreling, anyway."

"I wasn't the one who brought up the subject of the thefts . . . ," snarled Gombei.

The priest quickly interrupted. "Let's have a cold drink and calm ourselves." He gave orders to a young girl, who served them cold tea made from roasted grain, a refreshing drink on this hot, muggy day.

The girl served the two *ronin* first, and then set down two cups for Gombei and the ballad singer. Gombei, instead of taking the closer cup, picked up the cup that was next to the hand of the ballad singer.

Matsuzo noticed the action, and wondered if it had been an accident or deliberate malice. He watched the ballad singer stretch out his hand and then hesitate. But the hesitation was barely perceptible. Almost immediately he felt around for the second cup and grasped it. Matsuzo was impressed by how well the singer coped with his blindness. It made Gombei's spiteful action no less contemptible.

The priest seemed interested in the background of the two newcomers. "You are not na-tives of this region," he remarked. "Have you traveled this way before?" Under his lively brows, his eyes were bright with curiosity. He was really asking the two *ronin* who they were and why they had come to the valley.

Zenta gave a sketchy account of their most re-cent employment. As usual, he avoided talking about himself. The conversation then stayed away from the subject of the White Fox. Zenta seemed disappointed.

Soon the two *ronin* and Jiro rose and took their leave. It didn't seem as if they would learn anything more. As they passed through the *torii* gate and left the shrine, Matsuzo remarked, "I had the distinct impression that Gombei and the ballad singer disliked each other. And not just be-cause they disagreed about the White Fox."

Jiro chuckled. "They're rivals, because they both like my sister."

Matsuzo was shocked. "How can the ballad singer be serious about Kinu? He's blind!"

"That doesn't prevent him from liking a girl," said Zenta.

"You're right," said Matsuzo, instantly ashamed of himself. The blind had feelings, quite as intense as those of other people. "What does your sister think about the ballad singer?" he asked Jiro.

"She finds him entertaining," Jiro said airily. "Since entertaining people is his occupation, he should be happy."

Young boys can be cruel, thought Matsuzo. Still, if Kinu laughed at the ballad singer's jokes, that was better than scolding him.

They walked down the hill from the shrine and headed back toward the village. When one of the shabbier houses came into view, Jiro stopped and looked slightly uncomfortable. "I said I'd meet some friends here," he said to Zenta. "Can you tell my sister that I won't be back for lunch?"

Zenta regarded the boy for a moment. "I will, if you promise not to accept any more stolen goods."

Jiro shook his head vehemently. "I won't take anything that I'm not sure about! I promise!"

At their approach, a tall, wiry boy came out of the house. He looked about sixteen or seventeen, and he stared, frowning, at the two *ronin*.

"Hachiro," Jiro said to the older boy, "these two gentlemen are staying with us. Wait till I tell you about last night! They got me out of some bad trouble!"

The boy called Hachiro grunted a greeting that was just short of rudeness.

Zenta smiled and greeted the boy politely. "Do you also practice this new technique of jujitsu? I should like to see some more demonstrations."

Zenta's words floated in the air for a long instant. Hachiro stiffened and turned to glare at Jiro. "What did you tell him?" he demanded furiously.

Matsuzo felt almost sorry for Jiro. This was the second person to scold him for telling Zenta about jujitsu. He didn't see any reason for the extreme secrecy. Surely the valley people didn't expect to use the technique against Lord Yamazaki's armed soldiers!

"Jiro didn't tell me anything," Zenta said quickly. "I was hoping that *you* can tell me who your instructor is."

Hachiro glowered. For some reason he radiated hostility. "If Jiro didn't tell you anything, I don't see any reason why *I* should." He turned to Jiro. "Well, are you coming in, or are you too busy with your new friends?"

"I'm coming with you!" Jiro said hurriedly. He turned and looked at the two *ronin* for a moment. His eyes seemed to plead for understanding. Then he followed the other boy into the house.

4

"There was no reason for that boy to be so un-friendly," grumbled Matsuzo, as they walked on. "I wouldn't be surprised if he was among the ones laughing and jeering at us around the pool last night. Why don't we leave this valley and go to some nicer place?" His feelings were hurt. They had done nothing so far except help Jiro to escape arrest. Yet Hachiro, the older boy, had acted as if the two of *them* were the heavy-handed oppressors.

Zenta sighed and nodded. "Perhaps you're right. But before we go, I'd like to repay Kinu somehow. She's worried about the bad company her brother is keeping and she deserves our help."

"She seems to have plenty of helpers already," said Matsuzo. "She's got Gombei and the ballad singer. There may be plenty of other men dangling after her that we don't know about."

"Kinu is not the sort of person to have men dangling after her," Zenta said stiffly.

It irritated Matsuzo to see Zenta jump so quickly to Kinu's defense. What did he see in her?

They came to the stream they had followed earlier, on their way to the shrine. Zenta said he wanted to stop at the tofu shop and bring some back to Kinu.

The shop, an extension of the mill, had a room containing an earthenware stove with a cauldron for boiling the soybean milk. Next to it was a rack hung with cloth bags for draining the bean curds, and a table with some flat wooden forms for pressing and shaping the curds into tofu cakes. Some cakes were sitting in a basin of water, ready to be cut and wrapped up in bamboo leaves for customers.

The proprietor of the tofu shop was a small man with skinny arms that were nevertheless ropy with muscles. He seemed friendly when he saw the two *ronin*. "Are you buying some tofu to take to your hostess?" he asked. He evidently knew that they were staying at Kinu's house. News certainly spread fast in the valley.

"Yes," said Zenta. "We don't want to put a strain on her hospitality."

The proprietor began to make up the order. "Poor Kinu!" he said, as he wrapped the tofu. "She leads a hard life and there is a lot of sympathy for her around here. She was engaged to be married, you know. Then her parents and elder brother all died." He shook his head. "With only her and Jiro, it became hard to farm their land, so they had to sell a couple of their paddies. That was when her fiancé's family decided to cancel the marriage."

"What a shabby thing to do!" exclaimed Zenta indignantly.

"That's what we all thought," said the proprietor, glancing at him. "Gombei's family became very unpopular here..."

"Gombei?" interrupted Matsuzo. "*He* was her fiancé?"

The proprietor nodded. "He still likes the girl, but his parents were against the idea of allying themselves to a family consisting only of two poor orphans."

"How does Kinu herself feel about the broken engagement?" asked Zenta casually.

"She doesn't talk about it," said the proprietor. "She's trying to raise her brother by herself, and it certainly hasn't been easy."

"He seems to have a gift for getting into bad company," remarked Zenta.

The proprietor glanced around cautiously. "Some of the boys in the village are a little wild, and I'm afraid they will find themselves in serious trouble before long."

"Stealing, you mean?"

The proprietor dropped his voice. "Worse

than that. They've started to taunt Lord Yama-zaki's soldiers. They might get hurt one of these days. That's what Kinu is worried about, too..." He suddenly broke off.

They looked around. A middle-aged couple had approached the shop and were now staring at them. The man strode up to the two *ronin,* followed more slowly by the woman. "My name is Tozaemon," he announced coldly. "This is my wife. The tofu shopkeeper has probably been busy gossiping about us and our son, Gombei."

Zenta murmured his name. Matsuzo followed suit, thinking that Tozaemon seemed filled with both self-importance and defensiveness, an unattractive combination.

The tofu maker cleared his throat. "I wasn't talking about you, Tozaemon. I was telling them about Kinu and what a hard time she has been having."

Tozaemon stiffened. There was a definite re-semblance between him and Gombei. They had the same build and similar facial features. But To-zaemon showed none of the discontent Matsuzo had noted several times on Gombei's face.

"In these troubled times, we like to keep our eye on strangers visiting our valley," Tozaemon announced. "Of course it is not our business to be concerned with Kinu. Nevertheless her posi-tion is a vulnerable one, and we want to make sure nothing...ah...improper is happening." He looked at the two samurai, as if expecting them to account for themselves.

An insufferable man, thought Matsuzo. Even the tofu maker looked angry. It was Zenta who replied. "We've already learned that it is no longer your business to be concerned with Kinu," he said smoothly. "As you say, her position is vulnerable. People who had been expected to provide protection have forsaken her because she has become poor and had to sell some of her land."

Tozaemon drew back angrily. His wife had the grace to blush and look uncomfortable. Zenta continued, still speaking in a silky smooth voice. "We are her cousins, and we have come to give her badly needed support."

Several people hissed with surprise—including Matsuzo. Speak for yourself! he wanted to tell Zenta. For his part, he didn't want to be proclaimed as the cousin of a sarcastic young woman and her trouble-prone brother.

Tozaemon's eyes were now narrowed, and Matsuzo could almost see him calculating the financial condition of these prosperous-looking cousins. He might even be thinking that it had been a mistake to cancel the marriage after all.

At that moment an angry yell came from the back. A figure burst out of the shop and dashed toward the woods. Matsuzo set off immediately in pursuit. This could be his chance to catch the thief and prove Jiro's innocence once and for all. The fugitive was fast but Matsuzo was faster, and he was soon gaining rapidly.

Suddenly the fugitive stopped and whirled around. He was wearing a papier-mâché fox mask of the kind sold cheaply at many stalls, especially during shrine festivals. Recovering from his surprise, Matsuzo threw himself at the fugitive, who was unarmed, and grabbed. Without knowing how it happened, he overshot his opponent. He felt his arm and shoulder seized, and in the next instant he landed on his back with a thump that knocked him breathless.

As he struggled up, he heard sounds of mocking laughter from the escaping figure. It reminded him of the jeering he and Zenta had heard all around them at the bathing pool. Even more mortifying was the fact that the fugitive had the build of a young boy—perhaps someone even younger than he.

Zenta and the proprietor walked up to Matsuzo as he dusted himself off. The proprietor looked at the packet of smashed tofu on the ground and cursed furiously.

Matsuzo glared at them. "You don't have to tell me. I've just had a taste of jujitsu."

Zenta seemed thoughtful. "Does this mean that the mysterious and sinister White Fox is just a youth wearing a cheap carnival mask?" He sounded disappointed.

"Oh, no!" said the proprietor. "That was just one of the gang of village boys I was talking about. They put on a mask and pretend to be the Fox."

Tozaemon came around to the back of the shop. "I don't know what our valley is coming to! Instead of helping their elders with farmwork, these young people spend their time stealing and getting into trouble!"

"They've certainly developed a very effective way of hand-to-hand fighting without using weapons," said Zenta. He looked curiously at Tozaemon. "Do you know who is teaching them?"

"What gives you the idea that I might know?" demanded Tozaemon angrily. "I have better things to do than get mixed up with these young hoodlums!"

The assistant handed over a freshly wrapped packet of tofu and Zenta paid. The two *ronin* left, with the proprietor and Gombei's parents standing in front of the shop silently staring after them.

As they walked down the path leading to Kinu's house, Matsuzo rubbed the elbow he had bumped when he fell. "Do you still think the White Fox is some supernatural spirit?" he asked Zenta. "Or is he some jujitsu expert teaching the boys of the village the empty-hand technique?

Maybe he's organizing them into a rebel force against the occupation." He glanced around at the peaceful valley. In broad daylight it was hard to accept the supernatural.

Zenta said, "Maybe that thief is just someone who likes to eat tofu and doesn't feel like paying for it."

Matsuzo noticed that Zenta had not answered his question. "I've just thought of something," he said after a pause. "There are whole families training to be ninjas. They usually live in isolated valleys like this one, so they can practice their dirty tricks in secret." He detested the ninjas, for they used underhanded techniques no proper warrior should consider.

"It's true that more and more warlords have been employing ninjas," said Zenta slowly. "But they're mostly used as spies or assassins."

"Maybe jujitsu is just one of the skills they practice," said Matsuzo. He couldn't quite control a shiver of revulsion, for the ninjas seemed to have almost supernatural powers.

Zenta considered. "No, I don't think so," he said finally. "Ninjas always operate in secret, and their greatest asset is their ability to be virtually invisible. The White Fox, whatever he is, goes out of his way to make himself conspicuous."

Matsuzo wasn't completely convinced. As far as he was concerned, ninjas were an unnatural species, and so was the White Fox. The whole valley was unnatural. How could he persuade Zenta to leave this place?

When they reached Kinu's house, she was just boiling a pot of buckwheat for lunch. She accepted the tofu haughtily, but she could not quite conceal her relief at having something to supplement her meager supplies.

Zenta also gave her Jiro's message about joining his friends and not returning for lunch. She stopped stirring her pot and turned to stare at him. "Did he say which friends?" she asked.

"I saw only one of the boys," replied Zenta, "Hachiro, I think he was called."

"I was afraid of that," she said heavily. "Jiro admires Hachiro more than any of the others."

"Is Hachiro the bad influence you were talking about?" asked Zenta.

Kinu sighed. "He's just one of them. The boys have formed themselves into a gang here, thinking that there's strength in numbers. They have a romantic idea of starting a revolt against the occupation forces."

"At this rate, someone might get hurt," said Matsuzo, "and I don't think it will be one of the soldiers."

"Not if we can do something about it!" said Zenta. He looked at Kinu, whose distress was obvious. "Perhaps we can talk some sense into the boys."

Matsuzo didn't think they would have much success. "Hachiro and his friends don't seem to have any love for the samurai class," he remarked. The boy probably thought he and Zenta were here to enlist in Lord Yamazaki's army.

"I don't blame those boys for detesting the samurai," remarked Zenta, "if all the representatives they've seen so far consist of Busuke and his men."

"And Gombei," added Matsuzo. He glanced curiously at Kinu to see how she would react. He wasn't disappointed.

She stiffened at the mention of her former fiancé and started to speak, but then looked away and went back to preparing lunch.

"Gombei is different," said Zenta. Had he noticed Kinu's reaction? "He is a descendant of the Heike family, even if he grew up as a farmer."

"There is nothing wrong with that!" snapped Kinu. "We are proud to be farmers here in the valley. Without us, you samurai would starve!"

She served the buckwheat to the two men and thumped down Zenta's bowl so hard that he winced. Matsuzo almost laughed aloud at her directness.

Zenta meekly accepted Kinu's words. "Please

don't misunderstand me," he said. "I know the importance of farmwork, and I'd be glad to offer my help."

"In that case, there's still some weeding to be done in the rice field," Kinu said quickly. She grinned mischievously. She looked much more attractive when she smiled. "Jiro promised to help, but now that he's with his friends . . ."

"We didn't know you needed him," said Zenta. "Jiro probably just wants to play with boys his own age."

Kinu sighed. "You're right. I'm not bringing him up properly—as everyone here keeps telling me." With her shoulders slumped, she seemed very tired and badly in need of help.

Matsuzo could tell that Zenta was touched. "Of course we'll help you with the weeding," Zenta offered.

Farmwork is not what I'm trained for, thought Matsuzo. He almost ground his teeth with annoyance. They had money to pay for their food—only the confounded woman was too proud to accept any!

It didn't take long to finish lunch. The tofu was fresh, and seasoned with a few drops of Kinu's precious soy sauce, it tasted delicious. Matsuzo preferred to eat tofu with freshly cooked rice, but farmers like Kinu had to sell all their rice harvest and eat coarser grains, such as buckwheat.

As Kinu cleared away the dishes, Zenta said, "When Jiro returns home, we'll do our best to keep him entertained. Maybe he can teach us jujitsu and flip us on our backs. That should provide him with plenty of amusement."

"Jiro has other things to keep him amused," said Kinu. It was obvious that she did not want the boy practicing jujitsu with the two *ronin*.

She went to the door and pointed to a field with several small rice paddies. "With two of you weeding, the work should go very quickly," she said brightly.

They headed for the rice paddies. It vexed Matsuzo to see Zenta, his admired teacher, obeying the orders of a farm woman—even if she was a descendant of the Heike. "I didn't volunteer *my* service," he grumbled, as he glumly hitched up the skirts of his kimono and splashed into the muddy water of the nearer paddy. "*You're* the one who offered."

"Yes, but as Kinu said, the work should go quickly with the two of us," retorted Zenta. He didn't look much happier, however, as he squelched around, pulling weeds up out of the water.

"I'm not sure I can tell a weed from a rice seedling," muttered Matsuzo.

"The taller ones are the rice seedlings," said Zenta with a convincing show of confidence. He spoiled the effect by adding, "I hope."

Kinu came, looked at their progress, and nodded. "We'll make farmers out of you yet!"

As Matsuzo bent down again over the rice paddy, he found a shiny brown object stuck to his bare calf. "A leech!" he cried in disgust. Then he saw that it was only a dead leaf. Feeling foolish, he glanced up at Zenta and Kinu and saw that they were looking at two men coming down the road.

The men were samurai by their dress and arms. The deep straw hats they wore hid their faces from view, but one of the men was talking loudly. The voice was familiar. It was the one they had heard at the inn.

As the men walked past Kinu's rice paddies, they paused and stared at the two *ronin*. Zenta and Matsuzo had left their swords at the house, and as they stood barelegged in the water, they looked just like hardworking farmers.

The men dismissed them and walked on, still talking loudly.

Kinu made a sound of disgust. "They're all disagreeable, but those two are the worst!"

"They're part of the occupation force?" asked Zenta.

Kinu nodded. "That's Busuke, the one on the

right. He is the commander, and the other man is his aide."

Matsuzo looked at the way the commander swung his arms jerkily and pounded the road with his feet as he walked. Matsuzo guessed that inside the man there was a lot of roiling anger. It wouldn't take much to make the anger explode into violence.

"You can hear Busuke from the next valley," said Kinu. It was clear she was worried.

"You think there might be trouble with these two men?" asked Zenta.

Kinu didn't answer at first. "Our boys detest Busuke so much that they might try to do something foolish while he's here," she finally admitted.

The two *ronin* continued their weeding. The work involved constantly pulling their feet out of the sucking mud, and it drove Matsuzo close to mutiny. "We're samurai! Why are we spending our time farming? We've got enough money to hire somebody to do this work!"

Zenta pulled his hem out of the mud and tried to wring out the water. "We samurai shouldn't think of ourselves as being above farmwork. For all our high-sounding talk about honor, we're still nothing but parasites! We don't produce anything: We just wage war and kill people. The least we can do is help raise the food we eat."

Matsuzo sighed. Zenta had a point, but why bring this up now? He hoped Zenta wasn't suffering another one of his attacks of gloom. There was something about this valley that brought out the worst in people.

At least Kinu's paddies were not large. The two men, however inexperienced, managed to finish the weeding before the afternoon was over. Even in a good year, the rice harvest from this small plot must bring in very little money, thought Matsuzo, especially when there were only a young woman and a boy to do all the work. Small wonder Gombei's family had broken off the marriage arrangements.

Kinu came to survey their work. When she nodded approval, Zenta said rashly, "The work wasn't so bad."

Kinu smiled sweetly. "In that case, would you like to help apply the fertilizer?" She pointed to a wooden bucket sitting by the door of the outhouse.

Matsuzo shuddered. Even Zenta blanched. The fertilizer consisted of human waste.

Kinu laughed. "Don't worry. It's too early in the season for the fertilizer."

Really, Kinu has a very peculiar sense of humor, Matsuzo thought sourly.

In front of the house the two *ronin* sat down to wash their feet, while Kinu hung up some futons on a bamboo pole resting between a couple of trees. A small cloud of cotton dust rose as she shook the thin mattresses, and she began to cough. When she had hung up all four of them, she looked down the road. "What can that boy be doing?" she said distractedly.

"Perhaps I can go and search for him," offered Zenta.

Again, Kinu didn't spend much time being polite. "Thank you," she accepted simply.

As they fastened their sandals, they heard a rush of footsteps. Down the road came Jiro, running furiously. He arrived at the house and sank down panting in front of the door.

"Where have you been?" demanded Kinu, her voice sharp with alarm.

Jiro lifted his head. "They're after me!" he gasped tearfully. "But I didn't do it!"

Oh no, thought Matsuzo. Not again!

5

"Quick," said Zenta, pulling the boy up. "Inside!" Whatever happened, he thought, the blame seems to be falling on Jiro again.

Inside the house, Kinu stared at her brother in disgust and handed him a wet towel to wipe his face. "What has happened now?" she asked.

Jiro wiped his face and tried to catch his breath. "I don't know!" His voice broke and came out as a squeak. He swallowed and tried again. "I swear it! I didn't accept anything from anyone! I was just standing there, completely innocent!"

"When we saw you last, you went inside the house with your friend," Zenta reminded him. "Hachiro, wasn't it? What happened next?"

For an instant Jiro's eyes wavered. He bent down to straighten his clothes and tighten his sash. "We just talked a bit," he mumbled. "We didn't do anything."

"Then why are you rushing home like this?"

demanded Kinu. "You said somebody is after you. Who? The soldiers?"

Jiro nodded. "They started shouting at me, and said that I wouldn't get away with it this time." Some of his impudence returned. "I don't know what they're accusing me of, but whatever it is, I didn't do it!"

"Are the soldiers coming here?" asked Matsuzo. He went to the door and peered down the road.

"They might," said Jiro. "They seem to know who I am."

"If the soldiers come, I'll go outside and talk to them," said Zenta. "Maybe I can convince them you're innocent."

Jiro grinned. "You convinced Gombei and the other man last night that I didn't steal the dumplings. I bet you can convince them again."

Zenta thought Jiro was too optimistic. Gombei had his reasons for being lenient toward the boy, and he might not be in command this time.

It wasn't long before a group of men, armed to the teeth, came running toward the house. Things looked very serious. As the men came closer, Zenta could hear the loud, metallic voice. It was Busuke. If Lord Yamazaki's local commander came in person, then Jiro was being held responsible for something much worse than a boyish prank or a theft of dumplings.

The men stopped in front of the house, and Zenta stepped down to greet them. Busuke ignored his greeting. "Where is the boy?" he demanded.

Busuke had lost his hat and Zenta now saw his face. He noticed the man's eyes especially, for the whites showed all around the irises, giving him a fixed stare that made him look half demented. There was a big bruise on Busuke's left cheek, and Zenta could almost see it swelling.

He had to calm the commander, somehow. Violence could break out if he tried to stop the soldiers from arresting Jiro. Even if he won the fight, nothing would be solved. He and Matsuzo were only passing through, but Kinu, Jiro, and the other valley people had to live under the occupation of Busuke and his men.

"You mean the young boy who lives here?" Zenta asked, keeping his voice level and stalling for time.

"Of course I mean the boy, you idiot!" snarled Busuke. Spittle sprayed from his mouth. "Don't try to hide him!"

Zenta wiped his face and fought to control his temper. "What has the boy done?" he asked quietly. He hoped at least that Jiro would have climbed out a back window by now. He risked a peek back into the house, but Matsuzo was standing in the way.

"You're wasting my time!" cried Busuke. He turned to his men. "Go in the house and get him!"

Zenta placed himself in front of the door. "Do you have any proof that the boy did...uh... whatever it is he's supposed to have done?" He spoke slowly, drawing out his words. There was a scrabbling sound in the house. Jiro making his escape, he hoped.

Busuke barked at his men. "Cut down this fool and seize the boy!"

The men looked at their leader. They looked at Zenta. Slowly, they drew their swords.

Behind him, Zenta heard the faint hiss of Matsuzo's sword sliding out of its scabbard. "Put away your sword!" Zenta ordered him. "We can't start a fight!"

"You want us chopped up by that madman?" Matsuzo hissed.

"It's all right: Jiro's out the window now," responded Zenta. He had seen the boy's figure creeping away from the back of the house.

Unfortunately, one of the soldiers had seen him as well. "There he goes!" he shouted. Led by Busuke, the men started after the escaping boy, who ducked behind the line of futons hanging on the bamboo pole.

Zenta looked at the wall of thin mattresses, which Kinu had hung out to air in the sun. He had to prevent the soldiers from reaching the other side of the futons.

As one of the soldiers rushed at the futons, Zenta blocked his way and quickly ducked under the man's swinging sword. The sword whacked against the futon and raised a cloud of dust.

Leaving the soldier coughing, Zenta looked around to see what the rest were doing. Matsuzo was occupied with two of the soldiers. Zenta was sorry to see that his friend had drawn his sword after all, but at least he had avoided bloodshed so far.

If Jiro had any sense, Zenta thought, he would take the opportunity to run away as fast as he could. But the boy, out of pure devilment, raised one of the futons and made a face at the soldiers. "Here I am!" he taunted.

A second soldier rushed at him. But before he reached the mattress, Jiro's head appeared from under another one. "I bet you can't catch me!"

Zenta didn't know whether to laugh or groan.

With a howl of rage, Busuke lunged straight at Jiro with his sword. The boy fell back behind one of the futons. For an instant, there was dead silence. Even the soldiers stood immobile, shocked by their commander's violence. It was one thing to attack the two *ronin,* but running through an unarmed boy was a different matter.

The soldiers had been prepared to arrest Jiro, not to kill him.

Zenta swallowed hard, afraid to lift the futon and look behind it. Then out of the corner of his eye he saw a movement: Jiro, cautiously sidling away from the futon. He was not hurt!

"Run, Jiro!" Zenta shouted. "We'll join you!"

At last, Jiro understood his danger. He began streaking off along the road.

"There he goes!" screamed Busuke. "After him!"

Zenta knew what he had to do to delay the soldiers. Reaching up and grasping one end of the pole, he looked over his shoulder at Matsuzo and nodded his head.

Matsuzo needed no other signal. He reached for the other end of the pole, and with the pole held at shoulder height between them, the two *ronin* came at the armed soldiers.

This is just like reaping grain, thought Zenta, as they mowed down the soldiers in a wide swath. He couldn't seem to get away from farmwork.

As the soldiers coughed and tried to fight their way out of the dusty futons, Zenta turned to Matsuzo. "Come on—we'd better leave, too."

Instead of running, Matsuzo stood motionless, staring with his mouth open. Then he went into a violent paroxysm of sneezing.

Busuke finally struggled out of the writhing

pile of futons and rushed at Zenta with his sword raised. Still determined to avoid bloodshed, Zenta stooped under the slashing attack. Busuke bared his teeth, slewed around, and lunged.

Desperately, Zenta tried to remember how Jiro had used his jujitsu technique. He slipped slightly to the left, grasped Busuke's elbow, and pivoted.

It worked—partly. Busuke crashed forward and flopped over on the ground. But in the process Zenta felt a hot streak along his arm. He hadn't been able to avoid the man's sword completely.

Matsuzo grabbed his other arm. "Come on! What are you waiting for?"

"I was waiting for *you*!" snapped Zenta, starting to run. His arm hurt, and he was out of patience. As he ran, he did his best to tighten his sleeve around his bleeding arm.

Behind them, the other soldiers were regaining their feet. "After them! Chop them up!" howled Busuke's voice. "I want their heads stuck on poles and their bodies fed to the crows!"

Zenta risked a quick glance back. Busuke was in a perfect frenzy. His shouting had reached the point of incoherence. His men looked at each other and then at their commander, waiting for him to lead the way.

Busuke finally became too angry even for

speech. He simply jabbed his finger at the two escaping *ronin*. The soldiers began to lumber forward.

"Where are we going?" panted Matsuzo as
they ran.

That was the problem. They couldn't take
refuge at any of the houses, since the soldiers
would see them enter and follow them in. The
sun was now low. If they could elude the soldiers
until it became dark, their chances of escape
would be much better.

When they pounded past the place where
they had bathed the previous night, Zenta glanced
back at the steaming pool. A movement behind
the steam caught his eye: a flash of something
white. Then he heard a staccato bark.

"What was that?" asked Matsuzo.

From the cries behind them, their pursuers
had apparently seen something, too. Zenta looked
back at the pool again. The sight stopped him in
his tracks.

A white figure had materialized behind the
steaming pool. At first Zenta thought it was the
statue of a fox, for the head seemed to have
pointed ears. When he and Matsuzo were bathing, they hadn't noticed any stone statue. But then
the fog had been too thick.

The blurry white figure stood up and moved
slightly. Suddenly it turned, and an instant later it

disappeared into the trees. Zenta heard some sharp barks, which soon died in the distance.

"The White Fox!" cried one of the soldiers.

"It's only someone wearing a fox mask!" screeched Busuke, regaining his voice. "We'll capture him this time!"

The men didn't need to be whipped into action. They ran past the pool and into the trees, and soon the rustle of their passage died away.

Zenta and Matsuzo looked at each other, catching their breath. "Well!" Matsuzo said finally. "They've found someone more interesting to chase. I feel almost insulted. Where shall we go now?"

Zenta didn't have to stop and think for long. "We don't know the country at all. Rather than risk getting lost, we should head for the Inari shrine."

"Yes," agreed Matsuzo. "It's in a dense wood, so it's good for hiding. I think the priest would be sympathetic."

"Failing the priest, we still have the help of the White Fox," said Zenta. He didn't know what to think about that white figure that had materialized at just the right time. It seemed as big as a human being, but it definitely had moved on four legs when it turned and ran off into the trees.

Matsuzo glanced curiously at Zenta. "Now you'll want me to believe that the White Fox is a spirit who has taken us under his special protection."

Zenta didn't reply. He felt slightly uncomfortable, for what Matsuzo said was too close to the truth. He concentrated on hurrying.

"Well, whoever it was, we'll have to thank him when we see him next," Matsuzo went on. "I hope he escapes. He probably knows the valley a lot better than any of the soldiers."

"There's one soldier who *does* know the valley," Zenta said, as he tried to hurry. "Don't forget: Gombei is a valley man."

Matsuzo slowed down to let Zenta catch up with him. "But that's exactly why Gombei doesn't always agree with Busuke," he pointed out. "My guess is that Gombei won't let Jiro get into serious trouble."

"You saw the way Busuke attacked the boy just now," said Zenta. "He's dangerously out of control. Even if Gombei had been there, I doubt that he could have held him back."

Night had fallen by the time they reached the wood near the shrine. Zenta was now laboring as they climbed the hill to the shrine. His arm was throbbing, and he felt slightly sick.

He was also disgusted with himself. "I can't escape the feeling that someone had been planning all along to get us embroiled," Zenta said finally. "There must be some mastermind behind the scene who dealt Busuke a painful blow because he knew it would madden him and send him after Jiro. He also knew that this would force a confrontation between us and the soldiers."

Matsuzo did not look totally convinced. "You think the plotter actually wanted the two of us to be killed?"

Thinking about Busuke's wild fury, Zenta nodded. "The plotter might not want Jiro to be seriously hurt, but he fully intended to have the two of us removed from the scene—permanently."

Matsuzo smiled with satisfaction. "He underestimated our fighting skills—and the amount of dust in those futons!" he said.

Zenta didn't share his amusement. They seemed to be surrounded by enemies, and not just the soldiers. He remembered the mocking laughter around them during the attempt to steal their clothes and weapons at the pool. Jiro's friend, the older boy Hachiro, had shown unmistakable hostility, too.

They finally reached the *torii* gate at the entrance to the Inari shrine. Passing through the vermilion gate felt like entering a sanctuary. The soldiers seemed far away.

"Who do you think is teaching Jiro and the others jujitsu?" Zenta asked, as they started up the long flight of stone steps leading to the shrine buildings.

Matsuzo turned and looked at Zenta in surprise. "I thought we agreed that it was the White Fox! The tofu thief was trained in the art, and he wore a fox mask."

"And yet the White Fox appeared in person just now and distracted the soldiers," Zenta said thoughtfully. "So he wanted us to escape."

Therefore the White Fox was *not* the mastermind behind all this plotting to get them killed. It still wasn't clear whether he was the jujitsu expert, and responsible for all the thefts. Or even human.

Zenta began to feel dizzy. The trouble with this valley was that he couldn't tell friend from foe.

Halfway up the steps to the shrine he stopped. "I'll rest a bit here," he told Matsuzo. "You go and look for the priest. Perhaps you'd better sound him out first before telling him what happened."

Matsuzo looked concerned. "Is your arm bad?"

"No, just annoying," Zenta said shortly. "I'll leave you to decide what to tell the priest."

After Matsuzo had left, Zenta pulled up his sleeve and looked at the gash on his arm. It was long but not very deep, and the bleeding was already slowing. That was a relief.

The sun had set, and it was cool and dark under the trees. Sitting on a step Zenta finally had time to catch his breath and make plans about what they should do next. He still couldn't escape the suspicion that he and Matsuzo had been manipulated into acting according to someone else's plan.

Petty thievery wasn't a serious problem. The culprit would eventually get caught and receive a beating. A conspiracy against the occupation forces was a grave matter, however. Hachiro and his friends were definitely planning something. Zenta felt a shiver of alarm: If a simple bruise had sent Busuke into a frenzy, what would he do to the villagers when he discovered a full-blown rebellion?

So far Zenta's interference in local matters had been limited, and he had received only a scratch. But he couldn't abandon the valley people if they were in real danger from Busuke and his men.

Above all, he couldn't abandon Kinu. He felt a growing fascination for her, a fascination that was almost uncanny. She was not exactly beautiful, although her features were very fine. He admired her graceful, economical movements. Even when performing a humble task such as putting away dishes, she did not waste a single motion.

Her courage impressed him, too. More than

anything, he admired courage. He had met women warriors and had seen them fight valiantly and expertly with the halberd, the traditional weapon of samurai women. Kinu was no warrior, and yet she was just as proud and valiant.

Perhaps she didn't even want his protection. Or perhaps he should let Gombei do the protecting. But would he? The White Fox might also step in to help Kinu and Jiro. The trouble was that Zenta couldn't decide whose side the Fox was on.

Again Zenta's thoughts whirled around in confusion. He got up and slowly began to climb the steps again. Before he had gone more than half a dozen steps, he heard voices coming toward him. It was now completely dark under the trees, but he could make out the figures of Matsuzo and the shrine priest, who was carrying a paper lantern.

"Ah, there you are," said the priest when he saw Zenta. "As I told your friend, you are both welcome here. We'll make sure the soldiers won't find you."

They had guessed right about the sympathy of the shrine priest. More than just willing to shelter them, he seemed positively delighted. The light from the lantern showed his mouth stretched in a wide grin. His jiggling eyebrows seemed ready to fly off.

The priest led the two *ronin* to a one-room wooden building a short distance up the hill from the main hall. Peering into the room, Zenta saw several straw cushions and a low table. The place looked like the living quarters of someone at the shrine.

"We use this hut for visitors," said the priest. "The ballad singer is staying here at present, but tonight he's performing for some guests at the inn. I'm sure he won't mind sharing the room."

"There is no chance that he will report us to the soldiers?" asked Zenta. He had no doubts about the priest, but the ballad singer was another matter.

The priest laughed. The deep laugh had so much good humor behind it that Zenta's mood lightened slightly. "The ballad singer is nosy about everything that happens," said the priest, "but he never takes any action. He calls himself a blind spectator. Don't worry. You'll be perfectly safe with him."

He left and shortly afterward a girl came in with a basin of water and some strips of cloth. It was the same one who had served tea when they had visited the shrine earlier. After she had washed Zenta's arm and bandaged it deftly, she brought two trays of food.

It was a simple meal of rice, bean paste soup, and pickles. Matsuzo attacked it with gusto, but

Zenta felt little appetite. Nevertheless, he forced himself to eat.

No sooner did the maid remove the trays than the priest came back. "I have a visitor for you," he announced. "He has given his word that he won't report you, and I know that you can trust him."

The visitor was Gombei.

6

Gombei bowed deeply to the two *ronin*. "Thank you for helping Jiro to escape," he said. "I couldn't oppose my superior openly, but I knew the boy was not guilty."

When the visitor was seated on one of the straw cushions, Zenta asked, "I still don't know what the boy is supposed to have done this time. Is it connected with that bruise on Busuke's cheek?"

Far from being disturbed by his superior officer's injury, Gombei was almost smirking. "Yes, it is. This all started because Busuke is fond of eating *ayu*."

"The girl at the inn mentioned grilled *ayu*," Matsuzo said. "Is it a specialty of this region?"

Gombei nodded. "Yes, it's particularly tasty because of the special quality of our water here. Busuke saw some boys at a stream trying to catch the fish."

"So Busuke wanted to buy the fish from the boys?" Zenta asked.

Gombei's mouth twisted. "If he had, we would have avoided all the unpleasantness. No, he ordered the boys off and told them they had no right to fish in the stream without permission."

"That's outrageous!" cried Matsuzo.

Zenta agreed. He could imagine the indignation of the locals produced by such an order. "Many generations of valley people must have fished for *ayu* in the streams as their given right!"

Gombei nodded angrily. "The boys had to leave. What could they do against armed soldiers?" Suddenly he smiled. "Now, I wasn't present myself, and I'm just repeating what I heard from one of the men who was with Busuke."

"The soldiers were later attacked by little foxes?" asked Matsuzo, grinning.

Gombei looked smug. "The soldiers heard taunting laughter behind them, and they saw a group of figures, all wearing fox masks, making rude gestures."

"I suppose the rude gestures were used to lead the soldiers on," suggested Zenta.

"Yes," said Gombei. "The soldiers started chasing, and the figures escaped into the trees, but not before one of them gave Busuke a sharp crack on the cheek with a fishing pole."

Matsuzo laughed. "The soldiers have certainly had bad luck with bamboo poles today," he murmured.

Zenta began to have a premonition. "Jiro wasn't wearing a fox mask like the rest," he said.

"Ah, so you guessed what happened," said Gombei. "Jiro was the only one who was not masked."

Suddenly Zenta felt tired. "Where was Jiro? I take it he was found with a pole in his hands?"

"He was standing farther up the stream, still fishing," replied Gombei. "He ran away when he saw the angry soldiers, but they had already seen his face clearly."

After a pause, Zenta broke the silence. "You know what this means?"

Gombei nodded, no longer smiling. "The masked figures deliberately implicated Jiro."

He is genuinely concerned about the boy, thought Zenta. He must still be in love with Kinu, whatever his family had decided. He was not present when Busuke and his men came to arrest Jiro. What had he been doing at the time?

They heard voices outside. The door slid open, and Jiro stood outside with the ballad singer. The new arrivals had evidently been told about the two *ronin* staying at the shrine, but Jiro's eyes widened on seeing Gombei.

"You have nothing to fear from me," Gombei said quickly to the boy. "You should know that."

After a moment, Jiro nodded and entered the room. The ballad singer followed him in and closed the door behind him. The first thing Jiro did was bow deeply to the two *ronin*. "Thank you for helping me get away. I'm sorry that I got you into trouble, too."

"It's not the first time we've found ourselves in trouble with soldiers," Zenta told the boy.

"Yes, but that was the first time someone threatened to feed us to the crows," Matsuzo said wryly.

"I'd like to hear what happened," said the ballad singer. "I ran into Jiro skulking behind the tofu shop, and he said something about a bamboo fishing pole—or was it a bamboo drying pole? There are so many poles involved that I'm confused."

Gombei stood up abruptly and walked to the door. "The priest knows how to get word to me if you should need help," he said curtly to the two *ronin*. He nodded to Jiro and left.

"Now, why do I get the impression that Gombei doesn't like me?" purred the ballad singer. Far from being disturbed by Gombei's hostility, he smiled and adjusted the neckline of his kimono. Almost like a preening cat, Zenta observed. Did foxes preen and groom themselves? He brushed the thought aside. The singer was blind. Although Zenta enjoyed the man's humor, he decided that the ballad singer's constant flippancy could be irritating. Jiro was in danger from the frenzied Busuke, and that was not something to be taken lightly.

"Gombei is in a foul mood because he's worried about Kinu and Jiro," Zenta said. "And he has every reason to be worried, because someone here is deliberately trying to get Jiro into trouble!"

Zenta saw Matsuzo's surprised glance at him. Ruefully, he admitted to himself that he was getting heated. After a moment, another possibility occurred to him. "You know, whoever is trying to implicate Jiro may be planning to rescue the boy from the soldiers, so that he can earn Kinu's gratitude."

The priest laughed. "Well, it seems to me that *you're* the one who is earning Kinu's gratitude!"

"Explain how you got into trouble," the ballad singer ordered Jiro.

"Well, I was fishing by myself because I know a good spot," the boy began. "Then I heard a lot of shouting, and Busuke came running up with this big bruise on his cheek."

"And there you were, with a fishing pole in your hands," said Zenta. "Very neat."

Jiro nodded. "I managed to lose Busuke and the soldiers, but it was only a matter of time before they came for me." He looked at Zenta. "You know the rest."

"But *I* don't," complained the ballad singer. His curiosity seemed insatiable. "Tell me."

Zenta described how they had left soldiers entangled with the futons. The ballad singer's curiosity still wasn't wholly satisfied, however. "But it would have taken them only a minute to fight free of the futons. So how did you escape?"

"I know!" cried Jiro. "The White Fox came and rescued you, didn't he?"

Zenta nodded slowly. "You're right, he did. The White Fox appeared near the bathing pool, and the soldiers took off after *him* instead."

The ballad singer became completely still. "I wonder why he did that," he murmured after a moment.

"It's obvious!" cried Matsuzo. "He must be someone in the valley who is working to overthrow Lord Yamazaki's occupation. He wants to recruit us, so he helped us escape from the soldiers."

He turned to Zenta. "Why don't we join forces with the White Fox?"

Zenta was startled by his friend's complete change of attitude. Matsuzo had been the one who was reluctant to come to the valley in the first place and had argued for leaving as soon as they could. Now he was all for getting them even more deeply involved. "Well, I'm not sure . . . ," began Zenta.

"*I* am," declared Matsuzo. "I'm on the side of anyone who gave Busuke that purple bruise, and

against someone ready to kill a defenseless boy!"
With his warm and impulsive nature, Zenta
thought, Matsuzo is ready to forget Hachiro's
hostility and the mockery of the other boys. He
had become an ardent champion of the down-
trodden.

Zenta still hesitated. It was tempting to ally
themselves with the White Fox and help the valley people fight against their oppressors. The soldiers were after them, and the White Fox had
helped them escape.

But he still had the feeling that he had missed
something significant. Moreover, he didn't quite
trust the motives of the White Fox. "I don't want
to commit myself just yet," he said finally.

As he said this, Zenta looked around the
room and studied the others. Matsuzo looked
rebellious, but he managed to choke back his protests, just as he had on numberless previous
occasions.

Jiro's mouth hung open with shock and disappointment. The face of the ballad singer was
pensive, and his long, sensitive fingers caressed
the brocade cover of his lute. The shrine priest
looked completely blank. Even his lively eyebrows
were at rest.

In the stillness, Zenta heard some light rustling outside. He leaped up and swept the door
open. Nobody was standing outside. Feeling fool-

ish, he slowly turned back to the room and sat down again on his straw cushion.

"What's the matter?" asked Matsuzo.

"I thought I heard a footstep outside," said Zenta. "I was afraid someone was eavesdropping on us."

The ballad singer said, "It was the girl, getting water from the well. I recognized her step."

"I know I'm jittery," admitted Zenta. "It's just that this shrine is our last refuge. If Busuke and his men should discover we're here, there'd be no place left for us to go."

"It's different for you," Matsuzo told the ballad singer. "You're on good terms with everybody."

The ballad singer laughed. "Don't be so sure of that! As a matter of fact, Busuke is no friend of mine. I once sang some songs about his love of eating, using mock heroic verse."

"You didn't!" cried Matsuzo. "I'd love to hear them."

"You'll be sorry you asked me."

"I want to hear, too," said Zenta. He felt edgy and depressed. Maybe some entertainment would lighten his mood.

The shrine priest nodded, and his eyebrows danced. Jiro was almost jumping up and down in excitement.

The ballad singer needed no further coaxing.

He groped around for his brocade bag, loosened the drawstring, and took out his *biwa*. Watching the singer bend over to tune his lute, Zenta admired his sure fingers. The hesitations in his movements were so slight that it was easy to forget he was blind.

Finally the ballad singer picked up his plectrum and swept it harshly across the strings. Zenta recognized the introduction to the great naval battle scene in the *Heike Story*. But instead of a description of the desperate fight between the Heike and Genji forces, the ballad singer sang of the desperate battle between Busuke and a carp, which refused to stay dead on his dinner tray.

Zenta had to admire the singer's skill in preserving so much of the original heroic text. Spears became chopsticks, and spilled blood became spilled soy sauce. Jiro was sobbing with laughter, and Matsuzo was almost doubled over. Zenta tried to share their merriment, but his arm hurt and he was still oppressed by uneasiness.

The original epic ended with the annihilation of the Heike family, while Busuke's dinner ended with the death of the carp. In each case the ending was somber. By the end, Jiro was no longer laughing.

After the ballad singer put away his lute, Zenta turned to Jiro. "Does Kinu know you're safe?"

"As soon as Jiro arrived," said the shrine priest, "I sent one of the serving girls with a message for Kinu."

"She knows she doesn't have to worry about me," said Jiro.

"Jiro, worrying about you is your sister's principal occupation these days," Zenta said tartly. He felt a mounting tiredness. "It's late. Time for bed."

Jiro opened his mouth to protest. But he soon gave in and helped to unfold the futons from the cupboard and spread them out for sleeping. The room was not large. The four futons had to be neatly lined up with almost no space between them.

Jiro grumbled a little as he lay down, but went to sleep almost immediately. Zenta lay down between Matsuzo and the ballad singer. The latter was soon breathing regularly.

Zenta stirred occasionally, uncomfortable because of his arm. He found it hard to rest. He could not escape the feeling that he had jumped hastily to some unwarranted conclusions about the boys, about Busuke, and especially about the White Fox. This safe haven might be just an illusion, and they might be betrayed at any moment.

Nevertheless, until he got some much needed rest he would be unable to think clearly. He closed his eyes firmly and lay still, willing himself to relax.

———————

Lying on the futon next to the door, Matsuzo found himself wide awake. What should they do next? Zenta, being his teacher, should make the decision for the two of them. But he had refused to commit himself.

Matsuzo thought the issue was clear. He admired the proud spirit of the valley people. True, he had wanted to stay uninvolved earlier, but everything changed after he had seen the way Busuke and his men were abusing the locals. They wouldn't even let the valley people fish in their own streams! With his own eyes, Matsuzo had seen a troop of heavily armed men chasing down a thirteen-year-old boy. He had seen Busuke lunge at Jiro with a naked sword. Now he was ready to help the valley people resist the oppressors. He simply could not understand Zenta's indecision.

He also began to wonder about the true identity of the White Fox. Of course he was a human being, most likely a local man. Trying to recall the figure he had glimpsed at the hot spring, Matsuzo couldn't decide on its shape. Steam had obscured parts of the body. Since the figure had been squatting on all fours, he wasn't able to guess its height.

A fox is known for its cunning. Unlike a wolf, it does not always rely on the strength of its jaws. Therefore the White Fox, clever and skilled in ju-jitsu, did not have to be someone with a powerful physique.

An idea suddenly occurred to Matsuzo. Zenta looked tired and depressed and needed his rest. But he himself could try to meet the White Fox face-to-face! Maybe he could get an idea of what the Fox's intentions were, and if they were honorable, he could then convince Zenta that they should join forces with the resistance.

Of all the people in the room, Matsuzo felt himself to be the best qualified to act as a go-between and to carry messages from himself and Zenta to the White Fox.

He was sure that spies for the Fox lurked all over the precinct. Maybe one of them had made the noise outside that Zenta had heard. How could he get in touch with them? The shrine priest might help. Or he could simply go outside and make himself available. If they wanted to talk, they could come to him.

Having decided, Matsuzo got up carefully, in the smooth, silent way Zenta had taught him. He looked at the others. They were all motionless and probably asleep. Zenta had stirred restlessly earlier, but now he lay unmoving.

Matsuzo went to the door and tried to open it

silently. In spite of his care, he made a very faint grating sound as he slid the door open wide enough for himself to slip through. He quickly glanced back, but nobody in the room seemed to be stirring. As gently as possible, he pulled the door closed behind him.

Which was why he didn't see one of the sleepers open his eyes.

Once outside he let out his breath. So far so good. Treading gingerly, he headed toward the pavilion where they had chatted with the priest earlier. Matsuzo suspected that the shrine priest, with his twitching brows and his keen eyes, missed very little of what went on around him. He probably knew much more than he was telling.

Matsuzo didn't think he would run into any real danger. After all, the White Fox was an ally. Moreover, he himself was a fully armed samurai well trained in martial skills. The White Fox, for all his fancy jujitsu technique, was probably just a peasant.

Or was he? He could be a samurai, too. When the valley was occupied by the neighboring warlord, all the valley soldiers had been killed or had left for other masters. But one of them, giving himself a legendary name, could have come back secretly to organize resistance to the conquerors.

There was another possibility.... He reached

the pavilion and found it empty. The shrine priest had retired for the night, it seemed. Matsuzo sat down on one of the steps to wait. If the White Fox wanted to talk to him, he was ready to listen.

The summer night was pleasant, and a slight breeze cooled his cheek like a caress. The breeze carried a faint smell of pine needles, stirred up by the scurrying of some nocturnal animal. Matsuzo could hear small noises all around him—the chirping of a cricket, the hooting of an owl—the usual night sounds heard in a forest. It was so peaceful that he relaxed for the first time that night. He even began to feel sleepy.

A rustle roused him, but he relaxed again when it was not repeated. What had he been thinking about before he fell into a doze? Oh yes, there was another possibility. The Fox could also be one of the occupying soldiers, secretly in sympathy with the valley people. Perhaps he was even someone like Gombei, who had come from a local farm family and had gone off to become a soldier in the army of the neighboring warlord. But deep inside he was still loyal to the people of the valley. The idea appealed to Matsuzo.

He yawned, and found himself ready to return to the hut finally and get a good night's sleep. As he rubbed his eyes, he saw little moving points of light. Fireflies! He loved fireflies. As a boy he had occasionally caught a few and put them in a cage constructed by folding a sheet of thin white paper. The result was a tiny paper lantern, with the fireflies providing illumination.

As he stared at the bobbing lights, he realized that they were actually farther away than he had thought, and they were getting bigger. The lights were paper lanterns—not tiny toy lanterns containing fireflies, but regular lanterns with candles inside. He also heard voices coming from below, and he could now make out the sound of feet climbing up to the shrine.

Cursing, Matsuzo jumped to his feet. They had been betrayed. Busuke's men were here!

Who had reported their arrival? Could it have been the priest? But he had given them shelter. He was no friend of the soldiers, for they had vandalized the paintings in the pavilion and the statue of the fox. Surely he wouldn't have made contact with them.

It must have been Gombei! That treacherous villain had lied when he promised to keep their presence at the shrine a secret. Instead, he must have reported the news to his superior officer as soon as he left them.

There was no time to lose. He had to warn the others immediately.

7

Matsuzo ran for the hut where Zenta and the others were sleeping. The night was dark now, for the half-moon was behind the hill. Several times he stumbled over tree roots, and once he skidded on loose gravel.

Finally reaching the hut, he swept the door open and hissed a warning at the sleepers. There was no answer. Nobody moved. He peered into the darkness, and it took him a moment to realize that the room was empty.

He slumped with relief. The others must have heard the noise made by the soldiers and made their escape.

The ballad singer had little reason to hide from the soldiers, but Matsuzo was glad that he had gone as well. If he had remained, he might be questioned by the soldiers. Matsuzo didn't think it would take much pressure to make the ballad singer reveal everything he knew. After all, he owed no loyalty to anyone but himself.

The voices were closer now, and Matsuzo had to hide immediately. Where could he go? He didn't know the area and would blunder about aimlessly. The only comfort was that Lord Yamazaki's men hadn't occupied the valley for long and would probably blunder about as well. But wait— they wouldn't. They had someone with them who knew the area intimately: Gombei.

Cursing again, Matsuzo crept behind the hut and felt his way finally to a footpath. From the sound of the voices, the searchers seemed to have arrived at the pavilion. Matsuzo thought he could even make out Busuke's voice. It had a peculiar carrying quality. Why didn't the man speak more softly? Didn't he realize that he would lose the element of surprise? Perhaps Busuke didn't think he needed surprise since he had so many men under his command. Perhaps he was constitutionally unable to speak softly.

Matsuzo found himself climbing again. He was going up the hill behind the shrine, and soon passed through a series of small *torii* gates, only slightly higher than a man. Each gate had been constructed as an offering to Inari, in gratitude for a good harvest. Past the gates, he entered a denser forest, and it was so dark that he had to proceed entirely by feeling the ground.

Suddenly he tripped over something and fell. Suppressing a grunt, he got to his feet, realizing that there had been a grunt coming from the ground. He had tripped over a person—a person who was trying to keep silent.

"Is that you, Zenta?" he whispered.

Someone grasped his arm from behind, and he heard Zenta's voice. "That's the ballad singer on the ground. He was just trying to get up when you knocked him down again."

Matsuzo was acutely embarrassed at having knocked down a helpless blind man, and he could only stammer an incoherent apology.

"Don't worry," said the ballad singer. There was the sound of a rueful laugh. "I'm not at all hurt. Besides, I'm used to picking myself up from the ground."

That made Matsuzo feel even more guilty. He decided to change the subject. "Where is Jiro?" he asked.

"He went to the shrine priest," said the ballad singer. "The priest knows every corner of the shrine, and he'll have no trouble concealing the boy. He's also a very convincing liar, and he'll be able to mislead the soldiers, at least for a while."

Matsuzo thought about the shrine priest and his hearty laughter. That was a man who enjoyed a good joke. He would probably mislead the soldiers just for the fun of it.

"Too bad the priest can't find hiding places for all of us," said Zenta.

"But can we trust the shrine priest?" asked Matsuzo. He was a little uneasy about relying on a man who was a convincing liar.

"We don't"—Zenta stopped for a second, then continued—"have any choice, do we?"

There was something odd about Zenta's voice. He sounded almost breathless, as if he had received a slight shock.

"I don't think the soldiers are after Jiro particularly," Zenta went on in his normal voice. "*We're* the ones they're searching for now."

"It's Gombei!" Matsuzo said bitterly. "He must have told Busuke that we were hiding in the shrine!"

"You think Gombei was the one who told the soldiers?" asked Zenta. After a moment he said thoughtfully, "I can't believe that he would want the soldiers to seize Jiro, though."

Zenta has been completely taken in by Gombei's sympathetic manner, thought Matsuzo, which was understandable. The man had certainly given a convincing show of support for Jiro, for Kinu, and for his neighbors in the valley.

Perhaps that was why Zenta had been jolted. He had been shocked by his realization of Gombei's treachery.

"He's the only one who knows we're here," said Matsuzo. Gombei had never shown any particular warmth toward him and Zenta. If anything, there was always a stiffness about his manner. Matsuzo remembered the cold, calculating eyes of Tozaemon, Gombei's father. Like father, like son. Gombei would have no scruples about giving them away.

"Well, maybe you're right," murmured Zenta. He still sounded distracted, however.

"I'm glad you got out in time," said Matsuzo. "When did you people leave the hut? You went without telling me."

"We went without telling you," said Zenta patiently, "because you went without telling *us*. What were you doing sneaking around?"

"I wasn't sneaking around!" protested Matsuzo. "I thought I'd try to find the White Fox and tell him we're on *his* side."

"You *what*?" demanded Zenta. "That was an incredibly foolhardy thing to do—even for *you*."

"I don't see why," said Matsuzo hotly. "You're a fine one to talk about being foolhardy! What about all those times when we got into trouble through one of *your* whims? Besides, I thought we'd decided the White Fox *was* on our side."

"It may be safer to assume that the motives of the White Fox are unfathomable," murmured the ballad singer.

"How did you expect to find the White Fox, anyway?" asked Zenta.

"I thought if I sat near the pavilion, one of his spies would see me and report to him, and then he could come and talk to me if he wanted to," said Matsuzo. He sighed. "I guess he didn't, since nobody approached me."

"Then why were you gone so long?" asked Zenta.

"I must have dozed off," confessed Matsuzo. "Were you all asleep when I left?"

"Hardly," said Zenta. "You woke us by making so much noise opening the door."

"I got up shortly afterward to use the privy," said the ballad singer. "It was when I was coming back to the hut that I heard the approach of Busuke and his men."

"We'd better not stand here talking," said Zenta. "I can hear the soldiers getting closer."

"Our chances are better if we separate," said the ballad singer. "Together, we make three times as much noise."

Matsuzo was sorry to be separated from Zenta again, now that he had found him. Furthermore, he wasn't sure how they could arrange to meet later. But he could see the sense of what the ballad singer had said. "You're right. Besides, there is no reason for you to be involved with us."

Another faint laugh came from the ballad singer. "Busuke is no friend of mine, and I'd just as soon not meet him."

"You must have sung some pretty insulting songs...," said Matsuzo.

He stopped speaking, for he realized that no one was listening. The others had already moved off silently. It was so dark under the trees that he hadn't even seen them go.

Although he had just agreed with the suggestion to separate, Matsuzo felt abandoned. The question was, should he continue up the hill, or go down and take another fork in the path? Seeing tiny moving points of light below him, he decided to go sideways—off the path and into the trees. The lights got closer. He found a tall azalea bush and crouched down behind it.

Soon he could hear the sound of footsteps and voices again. As the light from the lanterns illuminated the path, Matsuzo put his head down, covered his face with his sleeve, and tried to breathe quietly. In this position, wearing a dark gray kimono, he hoped he looked just like a big rock.

Now the voices came so close that he could understand the words. "He said these *ronin* were dangerous." It was Busuke's voice.

Busuke must have been referring to the man who had betrayed them. It had to be Gombei.

"We should have killed those two men when we had the chance!" continued Busuke.

"*You're* the one who sent us chasing after the White Fox!" muttered one of the soldiers.

"Don't be impertinent!" shouted Busuke. "If I didn't have idiots like you under my command, I would have captured the White Fox *and* those *ronin* by now!"

Matsuzo wished fervently that the White Fox would come to their rescue again. The two of them were here in the first place because Zenta had gotten it into his head to investigate a rumor about fox spirits in the valley. Since the White Fox was a local hero, the least he could do was to appear again—and soon.

The lights were now very bright, and Matsuzo could hear the moving feet arrive at the trees closest to him. He didn't even dare to breath. His legs, tightly folded into a crouch, began to ache. A twig from the azalea bush had worked its way under the neck of his kimono and was tickling his back.

"But who are these *ronin*?" asked one of the soldiers. "They seemed to have materialized out of nowhere."

"They're just vagabonds," declared Busuke. "They must have come into our valley to look for work."

"They certainly are good at making themselves disappear right in front of your eyes!" said another soldier.

"Maybe they are fox spirits," said the first

soldier. His voice had a slight quaver. "Foxes can assume the form of humans. Whenever they wish, they change back into foxes and escape into the woods!"

Despite the cramp in his legs and other discomforts, Matsuzo had to stifle an urge to laugh aloud.

"Nonsense!" bayed Busuke. "You are soldiers, not superstitious peasants! Stop dawdling and start searching!"

"Just a minute," said one of the other soldiers. "Can you wait for me? I want to sit on that big rock over there and take off my sandal. I've got a pebble in there."

Matsuzo tensed. Would the man really come over to sit on his back?

"Idiot!" roared Busuke. "We haven't got time for pebbles or rocks! Let's go!"

After what seemed like an eternity, the steps moved on, although the soldier with the pebble was still grumbling. Matsuzo took a long, shallow breath of relief.

"I don't think we'll be able to continue searching for very long," said another soldier some distance away. "It's too dark."

"We have to try!" blared Busuke. "We can't let them escape!"

Matsuzo got up and took a few cautious steps.

Where should he go? At least he should head in the opposite direction of the soldiers. Their voices were receding at last.

He was just about to congratulate himself on his escape when he heard one of the men cry out. "What was that? There's a movement over there!"

The steps came pounding back in Matsuzo's direction. He hurried off the path and crouched down again, hiding his face.

"This way!" said one of the soldiers, who sounded alarmingly close. "I heard a sound coming from around here!"

"You're wrong!" cried Busuke's metallic voice. "The sound came from somewhere up that hill!"

"There's a rock over here," whined a familiar voice. "Can't I just sit down for a minute and get rid of that pebble? It's hurting my foot!"

"You and your pebble!" shrieked Busuke. "One more word and I'll chop off that foot! We're wasting time! Follow me up that hill!"

Matsuzo breathed again when he heard the footsteps finally retreating rapidly. The soldiers were running uphill. He raised his head cautiously, and saw that the lights were bobbing up and down on the path above him. The men were chasing after someone high above on the hill.

That being the case, the obvious thing for Matsuzo to do was to go downhill. He rose, and as the blood flowed again in his limbs, ten thousand insects seemed to be stinging him in the legs. He gritted his teeth until the sensation passed. He listened. There was silence.

Cautiously, he stepped in front of the bush and peered around him. Now that the lights from the lanterns had receded, he was enveloped in darkness again. Feeling his way along the path was difficult, but he didn't want to linger until the morning light made him visible to the pursuers. He hoped that Zenta had been successful in eluding the soldiers.

As Zenta climbed higher, the trees became thinner. Soon he could see the moon overhead. Only half full, it didn't provide good illumination, but it was better than stumbling along in utter darkness. At his back he could hear the voices of his pursuers. Since they carried lighted lanterns, they could run faster than he could. He was counting on finding a fork in the path, for he didn't want to be trapped into a bloody confrontation with the soldiers.

How had things degenerated so fast, anyway? Only a day earlier, he and Matsuzo had arrived in the valley with nothing but peaceful intentions. And now they were fugitives, with soldiers after their blood.

He was strongly tempted to leave this unlucky valley. The only thing holding him back was the thought of Kinu and Jiro. Zenta remembered the way Kinu had pushed Jiro off to bed the night before. She had tried to maintain a stern face, but for an instant her hand—fine-boned, though roughened by farmwork—had rested on the boy's shoulder in an affectionate caress. Zenta's throat tightened with pity and admiration for her, and he resolved to help her, whatever it cost him.

There! To his immense relief, he saw a fork ahead of him, the left branch narrower and barely visible. The main path led to the top of the hill, where there was presumably some secondary shrine building. That would be the obvious place to go. The other, narrower path led to places unknown. It took him only a second to make his choice.

At first the narrower branch seemed like a good choice. He heard the voices of the soldiers, and they either missed seeing the narrow path, or decided to ignore it, for he could tell from their steps that they were taking the main path up to the top of the hill.

After the sound of the soldiers had faded,

Zenta felt the weight of the silence pressing down on him. He had a strong sense of intruding into alien territory. He was tempted to clear his throat, hum a snatch from the ballad singer's repertoire —make some sort of noise to announce his presence. It seemed only polite to ask permission to enter.

The silence was broken by a dry bark.

He had heard that staccato yipping before. A fox, that was what it was.

He tried to recall the habits of foxes. Didn't they curl up in their cozy dens at night and hunt during the day like dogs or wolves? Or were they nocturnal animals with night vision like cats?

The dry barking was repeated. It sounded almost mocking. Foxes were mischievous animals and capable of cruelty. He realized that he was now thinking of foxes as they appeared in legends: supernatural beings who assumed various shapes and played tricks on people.

After a short distance, the path emerged from the trees, and in the pale light of the moon Zenta saw a sheer drop on one side. He was on the edge of a cliff whose bottom was out of sight in the blackness. He began to wonder whether he had chosen the right fork after all.

Rounding a corner, he saw that he was no longer alone. Standing in front of him and blocking his way were two figures. Each had the head of a fox, with pointed ears and a wide, grinning mouth.

Zenta could not quite control a shiver. There was nothing remotely humorous or friendly about the wide grins. He decided that courtesy was called for. "Busuke and his men are searching the shrine precincts," he said quietly. "I have no desire to meet them, and I should like your permission to remain here until the soldiers have left."

The two figures remained motionless and silent. For an instant Zenta wondered if they might be stone statues. But the two figures had human bodies. They were human beings wearing masks. They had to be!

A faint sound came from one of the figures, and Zenta knew for certain it was no statue. It was laughing softly.

He told himself that these were boys, only a few years older than Jiro. In fact he was sure he had seen one of them a short while ago: Hachiro. Only the masks gave them that eerie, unnatural air.

Zenta tried again. "Earlier today, while my friend and I were running from the soldiers, the White Fox appeared and distracted the attention of our pursuers. I'd like to thank him for helping us to escape."

Still no response. Zenta began to feel a stirring of doubt. "The White Fox *is* your leader, isn't he? You *are* taking orders from him?"

The two figures moved. They slowly turned to each other, and their heads tilted. Of course it is impossible to read the facial expression of a masked person, but sometimes the posture can provide a clue. Looking at the sagging shoulders and the opened fingers of the two figures in front of him, Zenta could have sworn that they appeared dumbfounded.

Zenta stared. What had he said that had so bewildered and dismayed them? Perhaps he had been completely wrong about the White Fox!

He was concentrating so hard on studying the two figures in front of him that he did not notice a third figure moving up behind him. By the time he heard the faint rustle, it was too late.

A hard push sent him over the edge of the cliff.

8

The bobbing lantern lights were coming back down from the hill. Stifling a groan, Matsuzo retired back into the trees, crouched down behind a bush, and again assumed the shape of a rock.

He heard the soldiers talk as they went past. "I told you there was nobody up there!" complained one voice. "What a waste of time!"

"Don't be a fool!" barked Busuke. "Of course we had to make sure! Now we know that they must have escaped to the village. We'll find them even if we have to search every household in the valley!"

None of the searchers he had heard so far sounded like Gombei, Matsuzo suddenly realized. Was it because he wasn't taking part in the search?

Raising his head at last, Matsuzo sighed with relief as he saw the lanterns recede down the hill toward the entrance of the shrine. He hoped it would be the last time this night he had to hide from the soldiers.

Or what is left of the night, he thought, getting up to stretch. He sat down against a tree and yawned in a tide of sleepiness. Where was Zenta? He must have managed to escape, for he was always resourceful. Tonight, though, he had seemed rather out of sorts. Something beside his wounded arm was bothering him. Maybe he had had a premonition that Gombei would betray them.

Well, they had foiled Gombei. They had succeeded in making their escape. They could now relax. . . .

Something made him open his eyes. To his amazement, he saw that it was no longer dark. Dawn had arrived, which meant that he had actually fallen asleep—what's more, he'd been asleep for some time. He sat up, looked around, and froze.

In front of him on the path were two figures with the heads of foxes. They were utterly still as they stood looking down at him.

Matsuzo sprang to his feet with his hand on his sword. He was much too slow, for his limbs were stiff from the chilly night air. If these foxes had meant to attack him, he would have done little to help himself. But they stayed motionless on the path.

Matsuzo cleared his throat. "Have the soldiers all left the shrine?"

For a moment it looked as if he wouldn't get a reply. Then one of the foxes moved forward. He was the shorter one, although neither was extremely tall. "They have all gone, and it is now safe for you to go down," he said.

The voice sounded strange. It could be the effect of the mask, of course. In the daylight, Matsuzo could see that these figures both wore papier-mâché masks, like the tofu thief he had grappled with. One of them might even *be* that thief.

But the voice also sounded very high, almost falsetto, so the speaker must be doing it deliberately as a disguise. These foxes didn't trust him completely just yet.

Suddenly the two foxes bowed deeply. For an instant Matsuzo thought that he had won their respect. Then he realized that they were not bowing to him, but to someone coming down the path. He turned, and his heart stopped for an instant.

Standing on the path was a figure all in white, and on its head was no papier-mâché mask, but a painted wooden one of exquisite workmanship. It was polished and gleaming with a soft pink glow in the morning light, and its mouth was stretched in a wide grin that looked somehow gentle and understanding, not derisive like the grin on the cheaper masks.

The White Fox himself had arrived, the master of the two smaller figures. Matsuzo had the feeling that this was the master of all the foxes in the valley, both human and animal. When the Fox appeared at the bathing pool to distract the attention of the soldiers, he had moved on all four feet like an animal. Now he was standing upright. Although not exceptionally tall or heavily built, he radiated confidence and power.

Matsuzo managed a graceful bow. "I want to thank you for helping us to escape. I also wish to say that I'm in complete sympathy with what you are trying to do in this valley. Please tell me what I can do to help."

The White Fox bent his head in acknowledgment. With the light shifting on the mask, its expression seemed to change. Suddenly it looked a little less benign and much more cunning.

"We appreciate your sympathy," said the White Fox. His voice was unnaturally high as well, and could be either male or female. "We will take full advantage of your help."

Matsuzo arranged his swords in his sash and stood straight. "Tell me what I can do."

He wished Zenta were here to see that he had been right after all. They could now work together for the White Fox and help the people of the valley to overcome their oppressors.

Zenta heard the chittering of birds. He opened his eyes to daylight and saw the soft, blurry outline of a tree branch above his head. It was early morning, and the air was misty.

He took a deep breath, and a searing pain went through his chest like a knife. He was sure his lung was punctured. But when he took a careful shallow breath, the pain was less, and the fact that he could control his breathing meant his lungs were intact. The pain was coming from a cracked or broken rib.

He tried to get up and assess the damage. The movement immediately caused several different troubled areas to clamor for attention. He closed his eyes for a minute and decided to wait before making another attempt to get up.

The last thing he remembered was being pushed off the cliff by someone coming from behind. He had a confused memory of loose rocks and scratching branches, before crashing into the trunk of a tree. One day, he would have to find that tree again and place an offering at its foot. It might have cracked a rib, but it had broken his fall and saved his life.

He gritted his teeth and pushed himself up on his elbows. His ribs screamed, and a gong went off in his right temple. Some portions of his shins appeared to have caught fire. But at least all his limbs worked.

Overhead, there was silence. It appeared that his attackers—or a single attacker?—had been satisfied of his end and had gone away.

To struggle up, he had to ignore an insistent inner voice telling him that it was much easier just to lie back and gaze at the sky. Finally, after what seemed like many hours, he succeeded in getting to his feet. When his dizziness passed, he looked about and examined his surroundings.

He had fallen into a ravine, and judging from the splashing sound, he was very close to a small waterfall, which he found after parting some branches tangled with wild wisteria. At the sight, he swallowed. On either side of the waterfall were big boulders, which he had narrowly missed in his fall. If he had landed on one of those, he would now be bloody pulp.

Suddenly he felt a raging thirst. Cupping his hands, he caught some of the cool water and drank greedily. Then he wetted his sleeve and used it to dab at the lump on his temple. This set off the gong again. He ignored the throbbing in his head and bent over to wash the scrapes on his legs. They could fester if they weren't cleansed. He saw to his relief that the fall hadn't caused the cut on his arm to open again.

High overhead he heard the sound of swallows. Looking at these swooping, graceful birds cheered him and gave him strength. All he had to do was get out of the ravine and find Matsuzo. Or perhaps he could go to Kinu's house.

The program was modest enough, but carrying it out turned out to be another matter. Pushing his way through the tangled underbrush caused his ribs to protest indignantly. The effort also made him pant, which his ribs liked no better. The only thing to do was to divorce his mind from the physical discomforts and think about how and why he found himself in the present predicament.

He and Matsuzo had been foolish to think that the foxes were friendly. They were treacherous, and they were trained in a fighting technique whose very essence was deception. He had overlooked the fact that some, or all, of them were thieves. Because the White Fox had helped him to escape the soldiers, he had assumed that all the foxes would help. It wasn't even clear that the others were followers of the White Fox, or completely under his control.

Zenta still didn't understand what the White

Fox hoped to achieve by the disguise and the thefts. Surely he didn't believe he could drive away Lord Yamazaki's men by playing the role of a local legend and stealing some tofu! Last night Zenta had expressed his distrust of the White Fox. His doubts this morning had increased considerably.

He decided to follow the small stream that started below the waterfall and meandered through the ravine. The disadvantage of this plan was that he kept slipping into the stream and wetting his feet. The advantage was that he had a constant supply of fresh water to drink. Moreover, the stream was getting wider and presumably led somewhere.... Although it might lead him back into the village and right into the arms of the soldiers. Or it might lead him to some totally strange locality. Since climbing the hill above the shrine last night, he had lost his sense of direction.

He had also lost his sense of time. He felt as if he had spent a whole day in the ravine, but looking at the sun he knew it was still morning.

Finally, the banks on either side of the stream widened, and Zenta was able to walk without being hemmed in. Soon the stream passed close to a road. Peering carefully both ways to make sure that no one was in sight, he climbed up to the road. It felt wonderful to walk freely, without having to push aside bushes and vines and stumble over rocks and fallen logs.

It was still hard to keep trudging, for the road climbed steadily. After plodding a short distance, he realized that the view was beginning to look familiar: It was one he had seen only two days ago. He and Matsuzo had climbed this way just before reaching the inn. By falling off the cliff and pushing through the ravine, he was approaching the mountain pass from the back.

He was seized with a longing for some soft fingers to attend to his hurts. The inn at the pass would provide that, and it was only a short distance away.

But it was risky to go there since the inn was also the headquarters of Busuke and his aide. On the other hand, Zenta calculated, the soldiers would still be searching the shrine and the village for the fugitives. Moreover, Busuke and his men were at the other side of the valley and would have to go the long way in returning to the inn. They wouldn't be taking Zenta's drastic shortcut by coming straight down the cliff!

As Zenta stood and debated with himself, the inn began to seem more and more tempting. What finally made him decide was the sharp pain in his chest every time he took a deep breath. His ribs needed strapping, and his cuts and bruises

needed soaking in hot water and soothing oint-
ment.

However, in his present tattered and bloodied
state, he must present a very alarming sight to the
innkeeper and his staff. They might even report
him to the soldiers.

A solution came to him. He could pretend to
be a commercial traveler of some sort who had
suffered an attack by robbers—by robbers disguised as foxes, in fact. He would be regarded as
an innocent victim.

To be convincing, he would not be able to
wear his swords. They instantly identified him as
a samurai. If he wanted to appear harmless to the
people at the inn, he would have to arrive unarmed. He set himself the task of climbing up to
the pass. Just before arriving at the inn, he forced
himself to remove his swords from his sash.

For a samurai, discarding his sword was
worse than cutting off his right arm: It was like
cutting off his soul. He finally hid them under a
mossy rock, patting the dirt around it tenderly.
He strewed a few leaves over the dirt to cover any
signs of disturbance. He felt almost maimed.
Then, taking a last look around to mark the place,
he turned resolutely and headed for the inn.

He wasn't worried about being recognized by
the maid. When he and Matsuzo had passed the
inn earlier, both of them had had the upper parts

of their faces hidden by basket hats, normal head-
gear for travelers during the hot summer months.
Two days ago, they had strutted past like samurai.
This morning, he was a bedraggled figure with a
cloth bound around his head, and he staggered
like a man at the end of his tether. It wasn't even
acting.

The maid had just slid aside the front door
and opened the inn for business when Zenta came
reeling up to the entrance. On seeing his sorry
condition, she gasped in horror. "What happened?"

Zenta leaned against the door frame. "I was
attacked by bandits," he panted. "They robbed
me and left me for dead."

The innkeeper came bustling over. "Bandits?
From the valley?"

The maid helped Zenta to sit on the raised
floor inside the entrance. He winced when she put
her arms around his waist. "Oh, those monsters!"
she cried. "They've hurt you!"

"I'm not sure we can accommodate . . . ," began the innkeeper.

"Of course we can!" protested the maid.
"This poor man needs help!"

Zenta understood the innkeeper. "They took
all the gold I was carrying," he said, "but they
overlooked some silver coins I have."

The innkeeper nodded briskly. "Take him to

the room facing the garden," he told the maid. Looking at Zenta's muddy face and dirt-streaked clothes, he added, "Our guest will probably want a bath right away."

Although Zenta longed desperately for a bath, he might have to share the tub with other guests staying at the inn. To his relief, the maid told him, "Nobody else is in the bath right now. The other guests have all gone out."

Stepping into the tub was agony at first, but the hot water soon dulled Zenta's hurts. The maid helped to wash his back and hissed sympathetically at all the cuts and bruises. "Those monsters!" she said again. "It was bad enough for them to take your money. They didn't have to beat you, too!"

Zenta wanted to close his eyes, so soothing was the hot water and the girl's gentle fingers. "I got these scratches when they pushed me into a ravine," he told her.

The girl cooed sympathetically. Her voice had the soothing effect of a mother singing a lullaby, and he had to fight to stay awake.

What is Matsuzo doing? Zenta wondered. He would certainly appreciate the hot bath and the attentions of the maid. Surely he had escaped Busuke's soldiers by now.

Matsuzo had not wanted to visit the valley in the first place. Having eluded the soldiers, he might have changed his mind about helping the local people. Zenta hoped that he might even now be climbing back up to this inn.

After the bath, a physician was summoned to examine Zenta's ribs. Pronouncing them to be only cracked, not broken, he strapped them tightly. Zenta felt better and found himself ravenously hungry.

No other guests demanded the maid's services, and in a short time she returned to Zenta's room with his food. She set two dinner trays on the floor, one with grilled fish and several small dishes of boiled vegetables, and the other with rice, soup, and pickles. After the austere fare at Kinu's house, the dinner looked and smelled wonderful.

As the maid took the lid off his soup bowl, she looked at Zenta with eager curiosity. "What was the business that brought you to our region?"

For a moment Zenta's mind went blank. Then he remembered. While searching for work during his wanderings, he had once served as a bodyguard for a merchant. Now he tried to recall how the man talked, the sort of terminology he used. "My business is mostly in . . . er . . . commodities needed for . . . er . . . urban development in castle towns."

The phrase sounded convincing, and the

maid was duly impressed. "Oh, I'm sure you must be traveling on an important business trip!"

The maid was very pretty and Zenta enjoyed her attentions, but her curiosity was bothersome. To change the subject, he asked if other travelers to the area had encountered robbers.

"Until you were attacked, the road up to the pass had been pretty safe," said the maid. "I've heard of cases down in the valley, though."

Zenta pretended alarm. "My business takes me through the valley! Isn't anyone maintaining security in the area?"

"A troop of Lord Yamazaki's soldiers is stationed there," said the maid. "In fact their commander, Busuke, is staying with us."

"Where is Busuke right now?" asked Zenta, trying not to show too much interest.

"He and his men are down in the valley today," said the maid. "Apparently something happened yesterday, and they're still investigating."

Zenta decided to sound out the maid on the occupation force in the valley. "Did the people suffer much from the invaders?"

The maid refilled his rice bowl from a lacquer container and skillfully removed the bones from his slice of broiled fish. "Not more than usual, after a battle." She made a face. "But after all, why should the peasants care who lords it over them?"

Zenta held out his rice bowl, which the maid silently refilled. As he ate he felt a vague sense of guilt. The arrogant samurai ruled over the people with their swords, until they were driven out by another group of sword-wielding samurai, equally arrogant.

Perhaps playing the role of an unarmed merchant had made him think that way. Besides, something didn't quite fit. Why should the White Fox and his followers organize resistance to the invaders if things were no worse than they had been under their old lord?

"So the valley people have no reason to resent the latest invaders?" he asked carelessly, breaking off a bit of the fish with his chopsticks.

Surprisingly, the maid disagreed. "The people in the valley are funny. They're very proud, you know." Then she brightened. "Tell me more about yourself. Do you travel all over the country?"

Zenta found it increasingly hard to sustain his act as a merchant. He was sinking more deeply into his role than he had intended, and was beginning to feel he was tramping through a bog. As he racked his brains for more business terminology, he was relieved to hear the sounds of men arriving at the entrance of the inn. The maid would have to leave and attend to the new arrivals.

His relief was short-lived when he recognized one of the voices—the metallic, penetrating voice that set his teeth buzzing. Busuke had arrived much earlier than he had expected.

9

Zenta had miscalculated once again. He wondered why Busuke had come back so soon to the inn. Surely he couldn't have finished searching the shrine and every house in the village already!

Zenta quickly put down his chopsticks and rice bowl. Rubbing his eyes, he yawned. "I feel very tired. I haven't had any rest since the attack."

The maid got up hurriedly. "Of course! I'll make your bed right away."

She removed the food trays and placed them outside in the hallway. Taking out a futon from the cupboard, she unfolded it with practiced ease and quickly spread it out on the floor. It was much thicker and fluffier than the "rice cracker" futons at the shrine and Kinu's house.

Zenta stretched out gratefully and closed his eyes. "I think I'll sleep for a while."

"I'll make sure that no one comes to disturb you," promised the maid, and she slipped quietly out of the room.

Shortly, Busuke's unmistakable voice sounded closer, and Zenta heard a hiss as the door to the next room slid open. He felt the floor vibrate with the tramping of feet. It seemed that Busuke and one or more of the soldiers were staying on the other side of the wall.

"Are you sure Gombei will do a thorough job of searching for those two *ronin*?" asked a voice from next door.

"He'd better!" growled Busuke. "He hasn't done his share of work since coming to this valley!"

"He comes from this area," said his companion. "That might be why he doesn't want to do anything that could offend somebody."

"All the more reason why he should do the searching!" declared Busuke. "He knows the territory. Besides, it's about time he shares some of the ill will the locals feel toward us."

That explains why Busuke came back early to the inn, thought Zenta. The commander had become disgusted with the search and had passed the thankless job on to Gombei. If one of the local foxes attacked somebody with a bamboo pole again, this time it would be Gombei who would get it across his cheek.

"What's taking that maid so long to heat our drinks?" said Busuke. "She's always been a lazy slattern, but today's she's worse than usual."

"She was attending to another guest here," said the other man. "Some important businessman, who was attacked by bandits."

"Important businessman!" snarled Busuke. "We're the most important people here, and she'd better not forget it!"

Zenta could hear Busuke clearly, for the wall separating the two rooms consisted of *fusuma,* sliding panels made of stiff opaque paper.

He heard the door to Busuke's room open again, and then the faint clinks and clatter of bottles and dishes. "It's about time!" barked Busuke. "I thought we'd have to wait all day!"

The maid murmured something.

"I'm not shouting!" shouted Busuke. "If your businessman wants to sleep in the middle of the day, that's his lookout!"

Again the maid whispered.

"I know he's been hurt!" Busuke shouted even more loudly. "What does that have to do with me? I feel like going next door and giving him a piece of my mind!"

Zenta sat up. If Busuke came into his room and recognized him, things could become unpleasant. And he didn't even have his swords.

He looked around desperately for some concealment. There was none. The room contained only his bed, consisting of the futon spread on the floor, and its covers. There was no table, even, since the maid had served his meal on a couple of small trays. The only seating consisted of a flat cushion, which wouldn't conceal a mouse.

Then he caught sight of a lacquered clothes rack. It was waist high and had two arms extending out on either side. After his bath, he had put on the cotton gown supplied by the inn, and the maid had hung his kimono on the rack, with the sleeves thrust into the two arms.

Meanwhile, Busuke's companion was still trying to calm his commander. "Look, our *sake* is getting cold. And we're having that delicious *ayu* you like so much."

"You can keep your *ayu*!" screamed Busuke. "I'm going next door to give that fellow a thrashing!"

Zenta felt the floor shake as Busuke struggled with his companion. There was no time to lose. Zenta slithered across the room and arranged himself in a seated position behind the rack. He quickly thrust his arms into the sleeves of the kimono, and bent his head so that it wouldn't show above the neck of the garment.

He was just in time. With a swish and a bang, the sliding panel between the two rooms opened and Busuke thundered into Zenta's room.

Zenta held his breath.

"Where is he?" demanded Busuke. "Where is that confounded merchant?"

"He must have left the room to go to the privy, sir," said the maid in a soft voice.

Zenta could feel Busuke's vibrating frustration. He could almost hear the man's teeth grinding. A snarl came from Busuke, and for an instant Zenta was afraid that his topknot showed above the kimono.

Then came the soothing voice of the other officer. "Come on, let's go drink our *sake* before it gets cold."

There was another long pause. Zenta found his outstretched arms getting tired. He itched to give the bullying Busuke a lesson in manners. But he knew that if he injured the commander or his companion, Lord Yamazaki might send an army into the valley to massacre the inhabitants. There was no help for it: He had to endure Busuke in silence.

Finally, he heard Busuke's voice. "All right, all right, I'm coming."

The two officers moved back into their own room, and the panels between the two rooms were pushed closed. Zenta let out his breath in a long, soft sigh and took his arms out of the sleeves of the hanging kimono.

He was about to slip back under his covers when he noticed that the panels were not entirely closed. There was still an open gap about the width of a finger. If he crawled across the room, the men in the next room might see the motion. He had to resign himself to staying behind the rack. At least he could relax his arms.

"Let me fill your cup, sir," said the maid.

There was a liquid sound of wine being poured. This was followed by the slurps of someone emptying his cup.

"Not too bad," growled Busuke. "Here, pour me another cup."

Now that his neighbors were concentrating on their meal, Zenta slumped forward and closed his eyes. He even dozed for a few minutes, and the next thing he heard was the maid departing with the dishes.

After a period of silence, Busuke's companion spoke again. His voice was much softer, but the gap in the wall allowed Zenta to follow every word. "About that fellow who was attacked," said the officer. "Our robbers must be extending their activities. It's no longer just some mischievous boys in the valley."

"Are you sure it's the work of the same gang?" asked Busuke.

"It's too much of a coincidence that there should be two gangs working in the same area," said the other man.

"Those two *ronin* must have taken part in this latest robbery!" said Busuke. "We searched for them at the shrine last night. And all that time, they were here at the pass, busily robbing this merchant!"

"It seems our informant isn't as reliable as we thought," the other man remarked dryly.

Zenta waited impatiently for them to mention the name of the informant. To his intense frustration, they failed to do so.

"With those *ronin* joining the gang, it's certainly much more dangerous," continued the other man. "Maybe we should supply some protection for the man bringing the gold supply for our monthly stipend."

Zenta's eyes opened. What had puzzled him up to now was the motive for the activities of the fox gang. They seemed interested only in causing mischief and getting Jiro into trouble with the soldiers.

The mention of gold changed everything. Now Zenta could see a reason for trying to kill him: He might interfere with the attempt to seize the gold. But what was the connection with Jiro?

"Our carrier didn't have trouble fending off the robbers last month," Busuke was saying.

"Yes, but the attackers that time were unarmed peasants, and our man was a samurai. This time the robbers have the help of these two *ronin*."

"That's true," Busuke said slowly. "Twenty pieces of gold would be a great haul for the gang.

I'd better appoint an escort for the man this very afternoon."

If it weren't for his sore ribs, Zenta would be laughing at the irony of the situation. Both he and Matsuzo were doing their best not to become involved with the foxes and their mischief. And now Busuke was putting the blame for everything on the two of them!

For himself, he was perfectly ready to let the twenty pieces of gold go to pay Busuke and his men. Again, he wondered what Matsuzo was doing. In spite of Matsuzo's sympathies for the rebellion, Zenta was sure his friend would have more sense than to get involved with something as foolhardy as a raid on an armed escort.

After the White Fox left, the two smaller foxes seemed more relaxed. Soon they began to laugh and chat. Matsuzo realized that these were boys, probably younger than his own eighteen years.

They stopped at a secluded glade, and one of the foxes took out a packet of food. "Let's have something to eat," he said, pulling off his mask and sitting down on a rock. "I'm starved."

"I've got some water here, Hachiro," said the other boy, taking out a gourd. He removed his mask as well and sat down with a sigh. The time for concealment was over, and the two were speaking in their normal voices.

Matsuzo leaned back against a tree and looked curiously at his two companions, who looked about sixteen or seventeen. He recognized Hachiro. Earlier he had been sullen and hostile toward the two *ronin,* but now he seemed disposed to become more friendly. He even offered to share his food.

Matsuzo accepted some cold millet wrapped in a bamboo leaf. There was a pickled sour plum embedded in the millet to lend some flavor. "What, no tofu?" he asked.

Hachiro stiffened, but relaxed when he realized that Matsuzo had been joking. "We don't often get away with tofu," he said ruefully.

So it *had* been Hachiro who had tried to seize the tofu the previous day and used jujitsu against Matsuzo to defend himself. Matsuzo gave the boy a wry salute. Traveling in Zenta's company had forced him into maturity, but it was nice to be with boys closer to his own age again.

They ate up the millet quickly and passed the gourd around. Drinking and wiping the mouth of the gourd, Matsuzo looked at his companions. "I saw you yesterday with Jiro," he said. "Is he a member in your band of foxes?"

Hachiro's manner had been open and confident, but at Matsuzo's question he looked away.

"I'm certain Jiro himself wants to join our cause. He doesn't like Lord Yamazaki's men any more than we do. But Kinu is afraid he'll get into trouble if he joins us, and she still gives the orders in the family. He obeys her like a little boy!"

"He *is* a little boy," Matsuzo pointed out. "Are you sure you really need him?"

The younger of the two boys nodded. "A lot of people in the valley admire Kinu, because her father used to be the...uh...teacher here. Even now people...uh...listen to what she says."

Matsuzo noticed that the boy had hesitated while speaking about Kinu and her family. For some reason she commanded respect from the valley people, from Gombei, from the ballad singer, and even from Zenta. She wasn't a heroic-looking figure. Matsuzo had met women warriors with physiques almost as powerful as those of men. Kinu didn't look powerful or muscular. In her case, he thought, she might give way when attacked, but she wouldn't yield.

Suddenly he realized that this was exactly the principle of *ju*. Did Kinu practice the jujitsu technique of fighting?

"If we get Jiro into our band, the valley people will think that Kinu approves of us, and we'll have everybody's backing," said Hachiro.

This was a mature and sophisticated view of the situation, and Matsuzo didn't believe that the boys had formed the idea on their own. It must have come from the White Fox.

He looked at his companions and assessed them. Hachiro, with his grave and moody air, seemed mature beyond his years. Taller than his companion, he looked gaunt from undernourishment.

The other boy seemed much younger, although it was probably his trusting expression that gave that impression. Both looked thin but athletic and muscular. If the rest of the foxes were also in good shape and trained in their jujitsu fighting technique, they would make a formidable band. Matsuzo wondered, however, if they could really do much against a troop of armed soldiers.

"Have any of you trained with the sword?" he asked.

There was a hostile silence. "What do you think?" Hachiro asked sourly. "We're not allowed to touch weapons! That's why the White Fox said you might be useful to us, since you look like an experienced swordsman."

Despite himself Matsuzo was flattered. "I learned everything from my teacher, Zenta," he said, trying to sound modest. "By the way, he can be much more useful to you than I am. He's a superb swordsman! Too bad we got separated while escaping the soldiers last night. Have any of you seen him?"

Again there was a silence, but this time it wasn't hostile. The two boys looked at each other for a long moment. There was no mistaking the consternation on their faces. Finally the younger boy cleared his throat. "Yes, of course we'll try to find your friend. Until then, I hope you'll do your best to help us seize the gold."

Matsuzo didn't believe his ears. "Gold?" he yelped. "You are planning to seize some gold?"

Hachiro nodded impatiently. "You don't really think we spend all our time stealing tofu?" He made a sign to the other boy. "We'd better go to my house and assemble the rest of the gang."

As they went down the road back to the village, Matsuzo continued to protest. "This is insane! I can't believe you're serious!"

"You'll see how serious we are!" growled Hachiro. "Come on, we have to hurry. The others are waiting!"

Arriving at Hachiro's home, they found that half a dozen boys had already assembled there, and several more came as they waited.

Matsuzo listened with growing horror to their ambitious plans. They *were* serious about seizing a monthly supply of gold sent from Lord Yamazaki's castle to pay Busuke and his men.

"Our leader said the situation is different now that you're with us," said Hachiro.

This time Matsuzo refused to be flattered. "What on earth do you expect me to do? The gold is sure to be well protected, and I can't fight a whole troop of soldiers!"

"You don't have to," Hachiro assured him. "The gold is always brought by one man. It's true that he's armed with swords and a spear."

"What, no musket?" Matsuzo asked sarcastically.

One of the other boys took him seriously. "So far, we've only seen the man armed with his two swords and his spear."

"Our jujitsu technique is less successful against someone with a spear," said Hachiro. "For us to be effective, we have to grapple with our enemy. A spearman can keep us at a distance."

Matsuzo had an uneasy feeling that he could guess why the little foxes found him useful. "So you want me to keep the man busy, while the rest of you try to rob him?"

Hachiro beamed. "That's the idea!" He turned to the others. "See? I told you he'd be a real help!"

The soldier who had been selected to carry the gold was sure to be a formidable fighter. Matsuzo had learned a lot from Zenta, but he wasn't completely confident of his own ability to come to grips with a really strong swordsman. Furthermore, the soldier might decide to use his spear, and he had even less experience fighting a spearman.

He looked around at the circle of boys. Some, like Hachiro, were close to his own age, but several of them were younger. They looked at him hopefully. In this company he must seem like a respected elder. He couldn't disappoint them.

"All right," he muttered. "I'll do my best."

Hachiro relaxed, and the other boys grinned with relief. "Too bad Jiro isn't with us," said one of the younger ones. "He doesn't know what he's missing!"

He isn't here because he has more sense than the rest of you, Matsuzo thought. In fact, one of the things he disliked was the way they had tried to recruit Jiro. "I thought it was a mean trick to give Jiro the packet of dumplings, when you knew the soldiers would catch him with it," he said.

Even Hachiro looked uncomfortable. "Well, we were told that was the only way to make him join us. He would be arrested by the soldiers, and then we'd rescue him. He'd join us out of gratitude."

"Yes, but not before they've given him a hard time," Matsuzo pointed out.

"They wouldn't beat him up," said the

youngest boy. "We all know Gombei wouldn't let anyone hurt Jiro. He's sweet on Kinu."

There was some snickering, but it was good-natured. Matsuzo gathered that Gombei, in spite of having joined the occupation forces, was not really unpopular with them.

"All right, we'd better discuss how you're going to set up your ambush for the gold shipment," Matsuzo said briskly. "Does your leader have a particular spot in mind?"

Hachiro began to describe the terrain on either side of the road descending into the valley. He was clear and precise, showing a grasp of details impressive in someone so young. Of course Matsuzo knew that most of the information must have come from the White Fox.

Where was he, anyway? Why wasn't the leader himself here to give instructions to his followers? Whoever he was, he had cunning and enough personal charm to win over these boys. He also had access to information about the gold. Matsuzo wondered how he had obtained it.

Meanwhile, Hachiro was describing the exact spot where Matsuzo would emerge and confront the soldier. Again, the boy sounded like someone repeating orders from his leader.

Matsuzo tried to stifle his misgivings. Listening to Hachiro speaking crisply and fluently, Matsuzo couldn't put his finger on anything really wrong with the plans for the raid. But he had an uncomfortable suspicion that they were missing something essential.

It would be much better if someone cool-headed like Zenta were present. He would be a better person to confront the soldier, too. It was strange that Zenta was still missing. Where could he be? He must have escaped from Busuke's men, but he would never leave the valley without telling Matsuzo.

"Too bad my friend isn't here," Matsuzo told the boys. "He would be able to take care of the soldier with the gold. Are you sure you don't have any idea where he is?"

The boys looked at one another. Again Matsuzo had an impression of consternation. He turned to Hachiro. "You know something about Zenta! What did you do to him?"

Hachiro looked away. After a moment he said in a low voice, "We didn't do anything to your friend. He's somewhere in the valley. I swear it!"

The other boys solemnly echoed him. "That's right! We didn't do anything."

Matsuzo stared at the boys one by one, scrutinizing their faces to see whether they were lying. In the end he decided they were telling the truth, though not all of the truth. But he was unable to get any more information from them about Zenta.

IO

The next room was quiet. Zenta decided that Busuke and his companion had gone to arrange an escort for the gold carrier. He went back to his bed again and lay down to think.

Matsuzo is far too sensible to get mixed up with a raid on the gold, thought Zenta, but some of the local youngsters in the valley might be tempted. It was true that stealing gold was a big step from stealing tofu. But he had to remember that the little foxes—for that was how he had begun to think of the boys with fox masks—were far more ambitious than he had thought. They had framed Jiro for theft, and therefore they were certainly capable of malice.

They were even capable of murder. They had pushed him off the cliff with the full intention of killing him.

Could the boys really do all these things without an adult directing them? He tried to remember the face of the older boy he had seen with Jiro yesterday morning, the one called Hachiro. Jiro had mentioned that Hachiro had been beaten by the soldiers. The boy could have nursed his resentment and brooded on an opportunity for revenge.

Zenta wondered how old the boy was. He had looked no more than sixteen or seventeen. The other boys had appeared even younger.

Then Zenta remembered how he himself had been at sixteen. He had left home at fifteen, but he had already had a thorough training in the martial arts from first-rate teachers. By seventeen he was a toughened *ronin* who had traveled widely and had held many different jobs.

But did he have the cunning to organize a gang, train them in the esoteric jujitsu fighting technique, and plan raids on gold shipments? He didn't think so. Those things required thinking weeks or months ahead. Even if some seventeen-year-old genius of the valley had exceptional leadership qualities and flashes of inspiration, Zenta still doubted that he could plan so far in advance.

The White Fox, the leader of the gang, had to be an adult. This person, disguised as the legendary figure Zenta had seen only briefly at the bath, could be planning a raid right now on the latest gold supply.

Zenta still didn't completely understand, however, why the Fox had to involve a group of teenage boys. With his cunning and his skill at ju-jitsu, he shouldn't have to recruit the boys, who might leak information to some relatives in the valley. By forming his gang of youthful helpers, the Fox greatly increased his dangers of being un-masked. He would also have to share the gold with them.

Zenta tried to decide what he should do. From what he had overheard next door, there was a definite possibility that an attempt would be made next morning to seize the gold supply. Should he try to contact the White Fox and warn him that the gold wouldn't be traveling with just one man, but would be escorted by a troop of Busuke's soldiers?

Why should he help the White Fox and his followers at all? They had tried to kill him. Matsuzo had been right about the valley. He should find Matsuzo, and the two of them could go away and leave these people to their own well-deserved fate.

Then he remembered that Kinu had opposed the thefts, and that attempts had been made to force Jiro to join the gang of foxes. What would happen to them if a bloodbath followed the at-tempted raid? Kinu and Jiro were innocent and had nothing to do with the White Fox, but that wouldn't save them from punishment at the hands of Lord Yamazaki's men.

There was another possibility. The White Fox could even be a woman: Kinu. A woman was capable of mastering jujitsu.

No! He could not believe that Kinu would order her followers to kill him. Perhaps one of the boys had acted without orders from above and had pushed him down the cliff in a moment of panic. The White Fox might even be furious with his follower for the act.

He remembered something that had puzzled him: The White Fox had saved him and Matsuzo from the soldiers, and yet the two young foxes had been stunned when he mentioned the rescue.

Zenta came to a decision. Somehow he had to go back to the valley and talk to Kinu. Pushing back his covers he rose carefully and found himself feeling much better. The bath, the doctor, the tasty meal—they had all helped enormously in improving his condition. His headache had retreated to a distant corner to bide its time, and his ribs didn't bother him unless he prodded them. The various cuts and bruises were negligible. Cautiously, he went to the door, ready to summon the maid. But when he slid open the door, he found her already standing right outside.

She gasped. "Oh, you're up! I've brought a hot herbal drink the doctor recommended. It should help with your aches and pains."

He was touched. "I'm sorry to be giving you

so much trouble, especially when you have other demanding guests."

She blushed. "It was no trouble at all. The other guests have gone out, and I had some free time. But are you sure you should be up?"

Zenta nodded. "I've already been delayed long enough. I have to continue my journey."

The maid started to protest. "You need more rest. Besides, the ballad singer is coming. He is somewhat late today, but he's very entertaining. You don't want to miss his performance."

Zenta already knew that the ballad singer was entertaining. In fact, he was convinced that the man was a rogue. He was also clever and could be a useful ally when there was trouble. Zenta wondered if he could find an opportunity to talk to the singer and enlist his help.

On the other hand, the ballad singer knew Zenta was no merchant, and he might be mischievous enough to reveal the fact to the other guests. It was time to leave.

The maid gave in when she saw that Zenta was determined. She helped him dress and carefully brushed a last bit of dust from his kimono. Her concern was obviously sincere and rather touching, and he couldn't help noticing that she had an attractive smile. But her face showed none of Kinu's fine character.

At the entrance of the inn, the innkeeper looked up at Zenta and frowned. "What? Leaving already?"

Zenta knew he had to allay the innkeeper's suspicions. "I have to get on with my trip." He took some silver coins from his pouch. "I hope this money is enough. It's all I have left, I'm afraid."

Seeing that he was to be paid generously, and that no further payment was forthcoming, the innkeeper was all politeness as he ushered Zenta to the door.

"By the way, I heard the voices of some soldiers earlier," Zenta said casually. "Are they still around?"

"They should be returning shortly," the innkeeper replied. He peered at Zenta with a trace of suspicion in his eyes. "Why do you want to know?"

Zenta laughed lightly. "As long as there are soldiers in the vicinity, the bandits won't try to attack me again."

"Don't worry," said the innkeeper. "Busuke and one of his officers should be back at any moment."

In that case, thought Zenta, I had better leave instantly. The first thing he wanted to do was recover his swords. Being without them was like missing an arm or a leg. He lost no time and hurried back toward the place where he had emerged after climbing out of the ravine.

But he was already too late. Busuke's brassy voice sounded down the road, almost from the very place where Zenta had hidden his swords.

A bend in the road hid Zenta from sight, but even around the bend he could hear that Busuke was saying something about the escort for the gold. Zenta bit his lip in frustration. Now he would have to do without his swords a little longer.

He quickly reversed his direction and began the descent back down into the valley. Having passed this way once before, he was prepared for the steepness and was able to make good speed.

In a strange way, it was like a repetition of the previous descent. Twilight was approaching, and an oppressive quiet hung over the trees. Zenta couldn't help thinking of the warmth and comfort of the inn and the friendliness of the maid. It was hard to leave all that and return to this dank, hostile valley where people tried to kill him for no reason at all.

Yet something drew him to descend into the valley again. Although the mist was not as thick as last time, Zenta experienced the same chilling isolation and eeriness. In this place, he was almost ready to believe that the White Fox was more than a manipulative man in a mask, greedy for gold. He had always felt a compulsion to discover the true identity of a legendary figure, and whether it was really a supernatural spirit or merely a clever fake.

There! There was that dry, yipping kind of bark again. Whether it had been made by a man or a fox, he could not tell. His hand automatically went to his swords—and found them gone. He had only his wits for his defense.

The ground leveled out, and soon he saw Kinu's house again, its worn and sagging thatched roof gilded by the setting sun. A wisp of smoke stole around a corner of the house.

He approached, unsure of his welcome. He and Matsuzo—where was Matsuzo, anyway?— were hunted men. Kinu might find his presence an embarrassment now. But still he had to deliver his warning to Jiro, and to Jiro's friends.

"Is anybody there?" he asked, and it struck him again how he was repeating his previous actions.

Just the same as last time, Kinu came around from the back. She stared at him. Then she beckoned him to follow her inside. "Come in quickly, before somebody sees you."

"Don't worry," Zenta told her, as he removed his sandals. "Busuke and his men are up at the pass."

Entering the house, Zenta saw Jiro seated next to the fire pit. Beside him was Gombei. The latter had a gift for being where Zenta did not expect to find him.

If Zenta was surprised, Gombei was even more so. His eyes narrowed and he stared at Zenta for a long moment. "That looks like a nasty bruise on your head," he said finally.

Slowly, Zenta came forward, pulled up a straw pad, and seated himself. "I fell off a cliff while escaping Busuke's men. You didn't join the chase at the shrine?"

"I managed to get out of that," said Gombei. He smiled wryly. "Busuke ordered me to search the valley, though. As you can see, I'm not exactly rushing to obey his order."

Kinu brought over some bowls of hot gruel. "Gombei disagrees with Busuke about a number of things."

"Then I hope you disagree with Busuke about *me*," Zenta said to Gombei. "I'm too tired to run again tonight." He turned to Jiro. "Have you seen Matsuzo?"

Jiro shook his head. "Maybe he went with the ballad singer. Do you think they might be captured by Busuke's men?"

"No," said Zenta. "At the moment, Busuke is under the impression that my friend and I are busily working for the White Fox."

He certainly had everyone's attention now.

"How do you know?" demanded Kinu. "You've seen Busuke?"

Zenta had not expected Gombei's presence at Kinu's house, but he decided there was no reason why he shouldn't hear what had happened to him. "I'd better tell you everything," he said. He began by telling them about being pushed off the cliff.

Kinu stared at him with horror. "They might have killed you!"

"That was probably their intention," Zenta said dryly.

"What happened to your swords?" asked Gombei. "Did you lose them when you fell?"

Zenta hesitated. He felt a strong reluctance to tell the other man that he had hidden his swords. So far Gombei had not been actually hostile, and he was undoubtedly solicitous about Kinu and Jiro. But now his voice had an edge to it and his eyes had a hard glitter almost like animosity. Zenta wondered if it was possible that Gombei was jealous of him because Kinu had expressed so much concern about his fall.

Kinu was still bristling with outrage. "You call these boys your friends?" she asked her brother.

Jiro bit his lip. "My friends wouldn't kill anyone! It must be their leader who did it!"

"But why should the White Fox want to kill me?" asked Zenta, genuinely puzzled. "I haven't done him any harm! Since coming to the valley, I've had to spend all my time escaping from Busuke's soldiers!"

"Wait," said Gombei. "You're assuming that the White Fox is the leader of these local boys. How do you know that?"

"You think that the thefts were all planned by someone else?" asked Zenta. "Then where does the White Fox come in?"

"The White Fox is simply a local legend," said Gombei. "He may not even be a real person."

"But I actually saw him!" insisted Zenta. "I distinctly saw a white figure at the bathing pool, and it had the head of a fox!"

"I believe there really is a White Fox," Kinu said slowly. "But his purpose might be altogether different from what these boys think."

Gombei stood up. "We just can't seem to agree on this. I'd better leave before Busuke gets even angrier with me."

After Gombei had left, Zenta caught Kinu's eye. "There's something I'd better tell you." He described to her and Jiro how he had climbed out of the ravine and reached the inn. He ended by repeating the conversation he had overheard about the gold.

Kinu frowned. "Anyone who makes an attempt on the gold is going to get an unpleasant surprise."

"What do you think, Jiro?" Zenta asked the boy. "Will your friends try anything? Personally, I think they deserve a good thrashing. But they don't deserve being cut to pieces by a troop of armed men."

"My friends don't talk to me anymore," Jiro said in a low voice, turning away.

"I didn't want to mention this while Gombei was here," said Zenta. "His position is an awkward one. Busuke is his commanding officer, so theoretically he should be reporting anything suspicious to him."

Kinu looked her brother in the eye. "Jiro, you have to tell me the truth: Are your friends planning to do anything about the gold? You must have some idea!"

"I did hear Hachiro mention something about the gold," Jiro admitted finally. "He thought it would be a great joke on Busuke if he lost his monthly allowance."

Kinu and Zenta exchanged glances. "Maybe that's why they tried to kill you," Kinu said. "They thought you might interfere!"

After thinking a moment, Zenta disagreed. "No, I don't think that was the reason they attacked me. They couldn't predict that I would overhear Busuke talking about the gold."

"I know you must blame the boys for attacking you," Kinu said to Zenta. "But I hope you will do something to stop them from trying to seize the gold. It would be terrible if they were hurt."

Kinu was pleading. For someone as proud as she was, it must have been painful to beg. Zenta nodded. "Very well. I'll try to think of some way to persuade them."

"Thank you," Kinu said simply, but her gratitude was obvious. "We should all try to get some rest tonight. I'd better take in the futons." As she went to the door, she turned around and said wryly, "I had a lot of rips to mend."

After Kinu went outside, Zenta looked at Jiro. "Can you accompany me while I talk to your friends? Otherwise they might attack me before I even get a chance to open my mouth."

"They won't listen to me," said Jiro, looking at the cold ashes in the fire pit. "They're angry at me, because I won't do what they want." He looked up at Zenta. "You don't know what it's like to be an outcast, when nobody is your friend."

"I *do* know what it's like," Zenta said gently. "I'm a *ronin,* a samurai without a lord, and that means being an outcast."

"But you're so confident!" said Jiro. "You're a good fighter, and your friend admires you."

"But I wasn't always confident—or a good fighter," Zenta replied. "I was thirteen once, although you might not believe it."

Jiro smiled weakly. "I liked the way you got those soldiers wrapped up in the futons."

"First we have to solve our immediate problem," Zenta said briskly. "How can we warn Hachiro and the other boys about the extra soldiers guarding the gold?"

Jiro sighed. "Some of the younger boys might listen to me, but Hachiro and the older boys will sneer at me. Besides, their leader is the one who gives the orders, and I don't even know who he is!"

An idea began to form in Zenta's mind. "Jiro," he said slowly, "I have a plan to help your friends. But first, can you give me some intensive lessons in jujitsu?"

"My sister wouldn't like it," Jiro said uneasily.

"She's the one who asked me to help," said Zenta. "Since I don't have my swords, I have to learn some empty-hand fighting techniques."

Jiro brightened. The prospect of teaching Zenta jujitsu obviously appealed to him. "I can give you lessons on either grappling or throwing techniques. Which shall we try first?"

Zenta grimaced. "My ribs are still too sore for

me to consider grappling with anybody. We'd better concentrate on some throwing techniques. I think that's all I'll have time to learn."

Jiro began tying his sleeves back. "All right. We'll start with some hip throws . . ."

11

Matsuzo lifted his papier-mâché mask and scratched the mosquito bite on his cheek. He peered around the boulder where he had hidden himself. The road was empty. It was likely to remain empty for some time, he had pointed out to the others. But they had insisted that their leader wanted them at their stations well before the gold carrier was due to arrive.

The leader. Why wasn't the White Fox here with his followers? The boys were being exposed to danger, while Matsuzo, an outsider, had the most dangerous job of all. And yet the leader himself, the planner, was absent. Matsuzo hoped fervently that the reason for his absence wasn't cowardice.

The sun had not yet risen, although the sky was a deep pink and it was bright enough to see some distance down the road. It was much too early to be up, especially after the wretched night he had spent at Hachiro's house. Kinu's futons had been thin, but very clean at least. Hachiro's mother had brought out—very grudgingly—a futon that was not only thin, but damp and smelling strongly of mildew. She was much too busy chasing after her errant son to spend time hanging out the futons in the sun, she had said with a sniff.

The family was too poor to afford mosquito netting or to burn the coiled incense that repelled mosquitoes, which was why Matsuzo was scratching the angry bite on his cheek.

More and more he was beginning to doubt the wisdom of this raid. If only Zenta had been there! He would have had the authority to talk the boys out of their plan.

Where was Zenta? For the first time Matsuzo began to worry seriously about his friend's safety. Whenever he mentioned Zenta's name, the others would look uncomfortable. Matsuzo was determined to make an all-out search for Zenta as soon as they had the gold. And he would force the boys to help him.

Matsuzo's stomach growled, and he grimaced. It would be a fiasco if his growling stomach betrayed his presence to the carrier. Hachiro's mother had been unable to feed her guest even a bowl of gruel.

It was understandable that Hachiro and the other boys would want to do everything they could to overthrow the new overlords. But would their acts of petty thievery do much good? Seizing the ten bars of gold was more ambitious, but it didn't really accomplish anything in the long run. The boys couldn't possibly hope to hire fighting men with the money. It might be enough to pay some mercenaries for one month, but to drive out the forces of Lord Yamazaki would require an army. Surely the boys could see that!

Matsuzo reproached himself for not pointing this out the previous night, during the planning session. Actually, he had not thought of all this at the time. The early morning air did wonders to clear one's mind. What was surprising was that the leader of the band, the White Fox, had not made more far-reaching plans. If he had, he wasn't telling his subordinates.

Matsuzo flexed his arms to keep them limber and tried to quiet the growling in his stomach. The sun was now gilding the hills, and it would shine right into the eyes of the gold carrier when he came around the bend. At least in choosing the spot for the ambush, the leader had shown foresight.

He had also made plans for how the young raiders should flee after they had seized the gold. Only a short distance away, there was an almost invisible trail leading down to a ravine, and by following a stream in the ravine, they would find themselves at the foot of the hill behind the Inari shrine.

Into the calm morning air came the call of the bush warbler. It was the signal they had agreed on. Matsuzo's heart began to pound. He was breathing faster, and steam was building up behind the mask, blurring his vision. He forced himself to take slow, regular breaths.

Soon he heard footsteps. But something was wrong: It was the sound of several people! Surely the boys weren't breaking out of cover before it was time! Had they forgotten their orders? Matsuzo was supposed to engage the gold carrier first, and while the two of them were busy fighting, the boys were to dash out and snatch the man's money pouch.

Matsuzo emerged from behind the boulder, and what he saw coming down the road made him gulp with horror. It was not one solitary soldier, but a troop of six men.

There may still be time to call off the raid, he thought. The boys can't possibly expect to succeed against this formidable escort!

Too late, Matsuzo realized that he was standing in plain view, and that he was wearing his fox mask.

The soldiers, catching sight of him, pointed

excitedly and began to shout. They whipped out their weapons and rushed toward him.

If only Zenta were here! thought Matsuzo desperately. He had never before fought against six men at once. He had learned valuable lessons from Zenta, and if these men were poor swordsmen, he might—just might—escape with his life.

But Matsuzo's hope was dashed when he clashed with the first man. It took all his strength to deflect the other man's spear, and he knew he was up against an experienced fighter. Even if all the other soldiers were second-rate, he was badly outnumbered and unlikely to survive.

When a second man joined the first, Matsuzo became too busy to worry, too busy even to despair.

Then something strange happened. Instead of joining their comrades, the rest of the men turned and ran the other way. One of Matsuzo's two opponents also ran off, and the other one looked behind him.

The distraction gave Matsuzo his chance. His downward stroke slashed the other man in the leg. As his opponent staggered, Matsuzo looked at what was happening behind the man's back.

He heard high, yipping barks and saw figures wearing fox masks swarming all over the road. That was what made the other four soldiers turn back. They began to attack the foxes with spears.

The boys must have known they were no match for the armed men, but they had rushed out anyway because they saw that Matsuzo was in trouble. Their gallantry was heartbreaking.

Matsuzo couldn't run to their aid immediately. He was busy with his own opponent, a very strong spearman who seemed little affected by the slash on his leg. At least the slight wound slowed the man and enabled Matsuzo to hold his own.

Now there were excited cries, and both Matsuzo and his opponent turned to look. Someone new had entered the scene: a figure all in white, whose fox mask was made of painted wood.

The White Fox himself had arrived at last. But like the boys, he was unarmed.

With a snarl, Matsuzo's opponent turned and ran to attack the figure in white.

Left alone, Matsuzo ran to join the rest of the combatants at the main scene of action. Just as Matsuzo's former opponent started to thrust his spear at the White Fox, one of the taller boys darted forward. Grasping the spear by the butt end, he tilted it suddenly so that it swung up just as the attacker thrust it.

As the spearman whirled around, the boy grasped him by the shoulder and pivoted him around. The spearman flew into the air and fell on his back. At last the boys were using their jujitsu! Before the fallen man could move, the tall boy wrenched the spear out of his hands, swung around, and raised the shaft of the spear to counter a blow from another of the soldiers.

Matsuzo admired the coolness and skill of the boy. He had to be Hachiro, the eldest of the young foxes.

Matsuzo had no time to see what happened next with Hachiro, however. He saw one of the younger boys threatened, and he rushed forward just in time to deflect a spear thrust from one of the soldiers.

In close quarters, the sword can be more maneuverable than the spear. Matsuzo defended himself without too much difficulty against the spearman, who was not as strong as his first opponent, fortunately. Where was the first man? He couldn't spare the time to look for him. He hoped that being flipped on his back had knocked the breath out of that formidable spearman and put him out of action, even if only temporarily.

Matsuzo reflected on the irony of the situation. This had been the role he was supposed to play: engaging the attention of the spearman while the young foxes robbed him of the gold. The trouble was that they had six soldiers to account for, not just one. Maybe there were only five left? Since Matsuzo found his present opponent relatively weak, he glanced around.

To his dismay, he saw that the spearman who had been thrown on his back was up again and was now using his sword. Neither the wound from Matsuzo's sword nor his fall could keep his former opponent down apparently. The man was a powerful warrior, and he had chosen to attack the tall boy, the one Matsuzo thought was Hachiro.

Matsuzo was surprised to see that Hachiro was defending himself quite expertly with the spear. Where did he learn to do that? This meant that some of the boys had received training in more than jujitsu.

Nevertheless, things were not going well. Matsuzo had less difficulty with his present opponent, but several of the smaller boys were under attack and he was too busy to defend them. Zenta! Where are you when I need you? he said to himself.

For that matter, what was the White Fox doing? He was an adult. He was the jujitsu master who had taught all the boys. He should be better able to fight the soldiers. But except for distracting the attention of the spearman, he seemed to be watching, keeping himself on the edge of the action.

Again, Matsuzo glanced quickly around at the boys. He was more and more amazed by the skillful way Hachiro used his spear to defend one of the younger foxes, as well as keeping his own opponent at bay.

Sensing a motion behind him, Matsuzo looked around just in time to duck and escape being speared through the chest.

Suddenly he heard a cry from one of the soldiers. "The gold! Someone has seized the gold!"

For an instant, everyone stood frozen.

Matsuzo took a sobbing breath. At least they had accomplished their mission. Now all they had to do was escape alive from the soldiers.

"There he is!" cried one of the soldiers. "After him!"

There was a flutter of white in the distance, and then it disappeared. The soldiers turned and ran after it.

Too spent to talk, Matsuzo and the others stood and looked at one another. There was no question about it: The White Fox was a master plotter. In one move, he had stolen the gold and drawn the attention of the soldiers away from his followers. Even the unexpected presence of the armed escort hadn't stopped him from carrying out his raid with dazzling success.

Matsuzo was confident that the White Fox would escape. He had a head start, he knew the terrain, and he could simply discard his white garment and mask. Once he had done so, he would look just like any of his fellow villagers.

"We'd better go," said one of the young foxes. The voice was familiar, but because of the distortion from the mask, Matsuzo couldn't tell which of the boys had spoken. None of them needed a second urging. They scattered, as they had already planned, each one going his separate way to reach the ravine. This would make it harder for their pursuers. And pursuit would be coming any moment, as soon as the soldiers gave up trying to capture the White Fox.

As Matsuzo scrambled away from the road and down the hillside, he heard a slithering sound above him. One of the foxes was coming with him. That wasn't too unexpected, since there were only a limited number of ways to reach bottom.

Thrashing sounds also came a little distance away from his right, made by one of the other foxes, perhaps. Or it might be made by one of the soldiers, since the thrashing sounded loud, even angry, with little attempt at concealment. Both Matsuzo and the other fox froze. After a while the noise died away, and they began their descent again. He noticed that his companion moved somewhat awkwardly. Maybe he had been hurt during the fighting. It was too optimistic to expect that all the boys would emerge unscathed.

It was hot work, climbing down the steep hill between bushes that scratched and branches that clutched. After a while, Matsuzo removed his mask. What was the point of hiding his face now? Strangely enough, his companion did not unmask.

After a while Matsuzo wondered if he was lost. The others had given him careful directions on how to get down the hill and find the ravine. He had passed the ancient bent pine tree they had described, and the moss-covered boulder. But pine trees tended to look alike, and one rock was hard to distinguish from another. He personally knew that it was even hard to distinguish a rock from a crouching man in a gray kimono.

He paused and looked at his companion. "You know the way better than I do. Are we on the right track?"

"I was hoping that you would know the way," admitted his fellow fox.

"But you're a local boy!" protested Matsuzo. "You must know the countryside!"

His companion stopped and seemed to be listening hard. It was quiet in their immediate area, although from a distance they heard the sound of several voices. "Well, I guess it's safe now," he said, taking off his mask and sitting down on a rock with a sigh of relief.

It was Zenta.

Matsuzo stared. "What . . . what are *you* doing here?" he stammered, when he finally found his voice.

Zenta mopped his face, which was wet with perspiration. "What did you think? I was trying to prevent those boys from getting killed."

"So it was *you*," Matsuzo said slowly. "I thought it was Hachiro! I wondered how he managed to become so good with a spear."

"I'm not sure I feel flattered," said Zenta, "if you mistook me for Hachiro."

"You could have told me you were there!" said Matsuzo, beginning to feel incensed. "I thought I had to fight those six soldiers all by myself!"

"How was I to know that you were planning to take part in the raid?" retorted Zenta. "I thought you had more sense! I was appalled when I saw one of the foxes fight with a sword, and realized it had to be *you*!"

"Where *were* you?" demanded Matsuzo. "Why didn't you come to the meeting when the boys and I were discussing the raid? Then you could have told us how insane the whole thing was!"

"The reason I didn't join you was because the boys tried to kill me," Zenta explained patiently. "They pushed me off a cliff in back of the shrine."

Matsuzo sat stunned. He couldn't have heard

right. "The boys pushed you off a cliff? I don't believe it!"

"Whoever they were, they wore fox masks," said Zenta. "This happened right after we separated two nights ago at the shrine, when the soldiers were chasing us."

Matsuzo's head was spinning. He still found it hard to accept what Zenta had said. Then he remembered that whenever he had mentioned Zenta's name, the boys looked uncomfortable. Suddenly he was swamped with fury. "You mean I risked my life and fought the soldiers in order to help those little fiends? I should have saved myself the trouble!"

He turned and stared at Zenta. "For that matter, you came to help them, too. Without you, we would have been massacred!"

"I don't think those boys are fiends," Zenta said quietly. "They have been misled."

"So how did you know about the raid on the gold?" asked Matsuzo. "And how did you manage to arrive just in time wearing a fox mask?"

"It's a long story," Zenta said in a tired voice. "I'll spare you most of the details. The fox mask I borrowed from Jiro. He got it when his friends tried to recruit him into the fox gang. Since everyone was masked, nobody noticed an extra fox at the last minute, especially when things became exciting."

"Exciting doesn't describe it!" said Matsuzo, shaking his head. "I nearly fainted when I saw those six soldiers!"

They were near the bottom of the ravine, and they climbed down silently until they reached a little stream. Thankfully, Matsuzo dipped his hands in and splashed his face. Zenta did likewise, and then they both drank the fresh, cool water.

"What shall we do now?" asked Matsuzo. He felt refreshed and ready to face new difficulties.

"I don't know," admitted Zenta. "Busuke and his men think we're the masterminds behind the raid on the gold. They will redouble their efforts to capture us."

"I don't see why they'd blame *us* for the raid," said Matsuzo. "There was an attempt last month on the gold, and that was before we even arrived."

Zenta sighed. "They're certain we're involved in this latest raid. They've seen you fight."

"But I was masked!" objected Matsuzo.

Zenta sighed again. "You used your sword. A mask didn't hide the fact that you fought like a samurai."

Matsuzo was silenced. They began to follow the stream, but froze when they heard some branches snapping a little distance ahead of them. When that died away, they moved on again.

"Did the White Fox give you any instructions about what to do after the raid?" asked Zenta.

"Hachiro said we're supposed to gather at the Inari shrine," replied Matsuzo. "If we follow this stream, we'll come to a trail that leads to the hill behind the shrine." He looked at Zenta. "But if the young foxes really tried to kill you, it's not safe for you to go. Where can you hide?"

"At Kinu's house," said Zenta. "Where else?"

Matsuzo looked at his friend. "Can you trust her?"

"There's nobody else in this valley I can trust," Zenta replied simply.

Matsuzo was doubtful. Zenta was not always reliable in his judgment about women. He, on the other hand, had grown up in a close family with three sisters and a loving mother. He felt himself to be far more experienced.

He had another uncomfortable thought. "There is one person who might have reason to kill you: Gombei."

"Because he sees me as a rival for Kinu, you mean?" asked Zenta. "That's too far-fetched. She hasn't shown any interest in me!"

"That was just a thought," mumbled Matsuzo. "You're right. It does sound far-fetched."

They tramped on doggedly. "We have to hide from everybody!" Matsuzo burst out bitterly. "Why don't we just leave this miserable valley? The young foxes got their gold, and we got the blame. So there's nothing to keep us."

They walked on. After a moment Zenta said, "What do you think Busuke and his men will do? Stealing a few pieces of tofu is one thing, but seizing twenty pieces of gold is altogether different. He will have to deal harshly with the valley people, to show them they can't get away with the outrage."

"Ten pieces," said Matsuzo.

"What do you mean?" asked Zenta.

"Ten pieces of gold—that was what the carrier was bringing," replied Matsuzo.

"Well, somebody has made a mistake," said Zenta. "I distinctly heard that there would be twenty. I heard it announced by Busuke's inimitable voice."

He peered intently at Matsuzo. "Who, exactly, told you that there would be ten pieces of gold?"

Matsuzo tried to remember. "Well, it came up while the boys and I were going over our orders last night. Who was it? I think it was Hachiro who mentioned ten pieces."

Zenta sat down heavily on a boulder. "Just a minute. Let me think."

"You think Hachiro was lying?" asked Matsuzo. "Or that somebody lied to him?"

"I was stupid not to have thought of this before," Zenta said, frowning with concentration. "I should have been wondering how the news about the gold reached the White Fox in the first place."

"So how did it reach him?" demanded Matsuzo. "Anyway, his informant was disastrously unreliable in this case."

"What a fool I've been!" said Zenta. He looked furious. "We have been manipulated by someone extremely clever!"

12

They saw Jiro standing in front of his house, looking anxiously down the road. When he saw them, he rushed forward. "Did you warn them in time?" he asked.

Zenta nodded. "Where is your sister?"

Matsuzo was surprised at Zenta's tone. It sounded grim.

Kinu appeared at the door. "What happened? Did you manage to stop the raid?"

The two men walked up to the house and sat down wearily on the front step. "We were too late," Zenta said heavily. "The foxes attacked the gold carrier after all."

Kinu hissed. Jiro went up to his sister and clutched her hand.

"But the boys are safe," Matsuzo said quickly. He didn't have the heart to prolong Jiro's agony.

"The White Fox succeeded in getting possession of the gold," said Zenta.

Jiro's shoulders slumped with relief. After a

moment his lips twitched. He couldn't quite hide his satisfaction at the news.

"Was anybody badly hurt?" Kinu asked anxiously.

"We managed to prevent anyone from getting killed," replied Zenta. "There were a few minor casualties, but none of the boys were hurt."

"I wounded one of the soldiers slightly," said Matsuzo. He couldn't help feeling pleased with himself. His former opponent had been a formidable fighter.

"You'd better come in," said Kinu. "We look like conspirators, whispering together like this."

When the two *ronin* had seated themselves, Kinu began setting out bowls of gruel. "You must be tired and hungry," she said.

When she served Zenta, he looked at her. "Why didn't you tell me about the jujitsu?" he asked quietly. "It would have made things much clearer."

Her hands froze. "I don't know what you mean," she said.

Zenta smiled faintly. "You're the expert in this valley, aren't you? You are the one coaching the boys."

Matsuzo nearly dropped his bowl of hot gruel. "But Kinu is a woman!"

Jiro laughed. "That's the wonderful thing about this technique. A woman can become an expert, too!" He was obviously very proud of his sister.

"But how did Kinu learn this technique?" asked Matsuzo, still incredulous. "I thought it was developed by Takenouchi Hisamori, and he must be dead by now."

Zenta looked at Kinu. "You learned it from your father, didn't you? You said he was a teacher of some sort. *He* must have learned it from Takenouchi or one of his students, and then taught it to you and others in this valley. When he died, you took his place as the teacher."

"My elder brother was supposed to succeed my father, but he died first," said Kinu. "How did you guess that I was the jujitsu expert here?"

"You kept stressing the importance of *ju* in coping with Lord Yamazaki's soldiers," Zenta said. "Also, Jiro is very, very good. He must have had the advantage of someone very close coaching him. But instead of being proud of him, you wanted to stop him from showing off his skills. Whenever jujitsu came up in the conversation, you tried to change the subject."

"Is that all?" asked Matsuzo. "That's not enough to prove that Kinu is the teacher. I thought it was the White Fox! That's why the boys respect him and take his orders."

"I thought so, too, at first," said Zenta. "In fact that was what had misled me for so long."

"So what made you think the White Fox was *not* the leading expert on jujitsu after all?" asked Matsuzo.

"I began to have my suspicions during the raid on the gold," replied Zenta. "Can you remember what the various people were doing?"

"Of course not!" said Matsuzo indignantly. "I was much too busy trying to stay alive!"

But now he cast his mind back to the raid. It was true that the White Fox had stood aside from all the action. The only thing he had done was seize the gold while the other foxes kept the soldiers busy.

"All right, maybe the White Fox doesn't know jujitsu," Matsuzo conceded. "But why should that mean that *Kinu* has to be expert?"

"What has been puzzling me all along were the repeated attempts to get Jiro in trouble with the soldiers," Zenta said. "It seemed so malicious and unnecessary."

"The White Fox, whoever he is, wanted to have Jiro arrested," said Kinu. "Then he could arrange for Jiro's rescue, and that would make me deeply obligated to him."

Matsuzo saw that Kinu was blushing. "So the White Fox is someone in love with Kinu," he said.

"He also needs her expertise in jujitsu," Zenta added dryly. "Since he doesn't practice the technique himself, he is afraid of losing the respect of the boys. But with Kinu at his side, the boys would stay loyal."

Matsuzo finally understood. He had been puzzled all along by Jiro's obedience whenever Kinu gave him orders, for it was abnormal behavior in a spirited boy of thirteen. Nor did Hachiro and the other young foxes dare to criticize Kinu. They all respected her as their jujitsu teacher.

"Tell us about the raid," said Kinu, changing the subject. Zenta described the attack on the gold convoy, and how the White Fox had managed to get away with the loot.

"What do you intend to do now?" asked Kinu.

"We're going to the Inari shrine," said Matsuzo. "That's where the foxes are meeting to divide up the gold they seized."

The skimpy meal served by Kinu was soon finished, but it was better than nothing and it stopped the growling in Matsuzo's stomach. As Kinu cleared the bowls away, they heard an angry voice. Although it still sounded very far away, they all recognized it immediately.

Busuke, having failed to find any of the raiders, must have decided to search the valley himself. This time he wasn't delegating the work to Gombei. He would soon be going through the village house by house.

"We should all go to the shrine," Zenta told

Kinu. "Your house is the closest to the road leading down from the pass, so it will be the first to be searched. We'd better hurry."

They lost no time in setting out. As they ran, they could hear Busuke's angry voice getting louder behind them. Kinu looked back anxiously. "They must be getting close to our house already. It will take them a while to go through the whole village. I hope Gombei stops them from being too brutal about it."

"Have the soldiers been brutal before?" asked Zenta.

"No, not unless they were provoked," replied Kinu.

"The soldiers beat up Hachiro," Jiro said grimly. "That was brutal."

"Yes, but that was because Hachiro had made a bow and arrow from some tree branches," Kinu said. "As long as we were not openly disrespectful, most of the soldiers left us alone. The boys were sometimes cheeky, but they were like that under the former regime, too."

Zenta grinned. "They were conscious of being descendants of the proud Heike, and they were not to be overawed by upstart warlords?"

Kinu was not amused, Matsuzo noticed. After a moment she nodded. "We don't have the power to oppose our rulers by force, but we suffer them as long as they respect our traditions."

Again, she means that the valley people believe in using the principle of *ju*, thought Matsuzo.

They had to hurry to get into the shelter of the trees before the soldiers noticed them. Moreover, the boys at the meeting might give up waiting for Matsuzo and start to disband. Zenta wanted to make sure that all the foxes would be present.

At the gate of the shrine, Matsuzo looked again at the two white stone statues of foxes. One of them seemed to be smiling.

Passing the pavilion in front of the main hall, they saw the ballad singer seated with the shrine priest. They were both motionless, and if Matsuzo hadn't recognized them, he would have taken them for statues, too.

The ballad singer raised his head at their approach. "You are going to join the meeting? It's in a clearing up the hill behind the hall."

Zenta stopped and stared at the two men. He stood there for so long that Matsuzo became impatient. Jiro, too, stirred restlessly.

Finally Zenta asked, "Do you know what the meeting is about?"

The ballad singer quickly shook his head. "I don't know, and I don't want to know!"

Matsuzo smiled to himself. The ballad singer hadn't changed. He might write a satirical poem about the gold raid, however, once he had heard all the details.

As they passed, the ballad singer called out. "Wait, I recognize that step. Is that you, Kinu? What are you doing here?"

Kinu stopped and turned to the singer. "I'm here, and Jiro is with me. This business concerns us as well."

The ballad singer froze once again. "Well, it's no business of mine," he murmured.

Matsuzo thought he detected a note of wistfulness in the singer's voice. He was amazed that Kinu, with no extraordinary beauty, could inspire such feeling in two men as different as Gombei and the ballad singer.

Matsuzo glanced back. The ballad singer had not moved. The shrine priest sat looking thoughtfully at them.

They found the meeting place in a small clearing behind the main hall. Apparently they had arrived just in time, for the boys were standing up and removing their masks as they got ready to leave.

It was childish and a little pathetic that the boys had put on their masks for the meeting when they knew perfectly well who the others were. Perhaps they felt that putting on the fox masks was a kind of ritual, part of being a member of the gang. Well, the masks suit their own purpose, thought Matsuzo. He adjusted his mask and saw that Zenta had already donned Jiro's mask.

The boys froze when they saw the new arrivals. Finally Hachiro said sourly, "We'd given you up. But I see that you managed to be here in time for sharing the gold."

"Actually, I don't want a share of the gold," replied Matsuzo. "We came because there's something all of you should know."

There was a stir when Zenta approached, wearing Jiro's mask. "Is that Jiro?" asked one of the boys. "I recognize the mask, but you're too tall to be Jiro!"

Jiro and Kinu, who had been standing behind the two *ronin,* now stepped forward. "No, that's not me," Jiro said. "Are you in for a big surprise!"

There were exclamations at the sight of Jiro and his sister. Hachiro turned and stared at Zenta. "Then who are you?" he demanded.

"Don't you remember?" asked Zenta. "When I saw you last, you were being attacked by a soldier with a spear."

Hachiro's eyes widened. "You're the one who wrenched the spear from that soldier! I wondered which one of us it was."

"We thought Jiro decided to join us after all," said another of the younger boys. "Afterward, when we couldn't find him, we thought we were just imagining things."

"So what are you doing here, Jiro?" asked Hachiro. "And who are your friends? We know Matsuzo."

"Since you know Matsuzo, you must know me as well," said Zenta, taking off his mask.

Some of the younger boys cried out, and then hurriedly covered their mouths. Even Hachiro looked shaken. "You . . . you are not dead, then?"

"I'm a ghost, come to exact vengeance from you," said Zenta in an eerie voice.

Several boys whimpered. "Of course I'm not a ghost!" said Zenta in his normal voice. "But I do require an explanation. Why did you try to kill me?"

"We didn't!" said one of the boys. "It was the White Fox who pushed you into the ravine!"

"You're betraying our leader!" cried another boy.

"This gentleman deserves an explanation," said Kinu. "He saved you from the soldiers. How many of you would be alive this minute if he hadn't helped you?"

It was clear that the boys saw the justice of Kinu's words. Finally Hachiro acted as spokesman. "I admit that our leader may have made a mistake. He told us that all the *ronin* are greedy, and that the two of you would take most of the gold, leaving only a couple of pieces for us."

Matsuzo was furious. Being accused of greed

by these little thieves was the ultimate insult. "If that was the case, why didn't he try to kill me, too?" he demanded.

Hachiro didn't meet his gaze. "He needed one of you to engage the spearman while we grabbed the gold. He thought that *you* were the more harmless one of the two."

That infuriated Matsuzo even more. "And after I have served my usefulness, he will order you to kill me as well? A man of honor and integrity, your leader!"

Hachiro flushed, and some of the other boys lowered their eyes. But nobody tried to deny Matsuzo's accusation.

"I think it's time to discuss your leader," Kinu said. "Has he said anything about what his long-range plans are?"

The boys looked at one another. It was obvious that the question had taken them by surprise. Finally Hachiro spoke up. "What do you mean by long-range plans? Our leader planned the raid on the gold. When the gold comes again next month, he'll think of another scheme."

Hachiro's innocence made Matsuzo want to shake him. Kinu, however, kept her voice even. "I'm not talking about the next gold supply. I'm worried about what the soldiers will do to the valley people after your raid on this one."

The younger boys looked puzzled, but Hachiro was beginning to show signs of uneasiness. "You think Busuke will take it out on our families?"

"Of course not!" Matsuzo said sarcastically. "After losing the gold, Busuke will go cheerfully back to the inn, take a bath, and dine on fresh *ayu*!"

"We valley people have never been thieves or bandits before," Kinu said. "Why should we start now?"

"We have to show our new overlords that we are a proud people!" Hachiro said hotly. "We have to tell them that we're not just dirt under their feet!"

Kinu's eyes flashed. "And to prove that we're not dirt, we steal food and household items? Attack a gold convoy?"

Hachiro opened his mouth, but after a moment he looked away and remained silent. When none of the other boys answered, Kinu continued. "We have lived under other masters for hundreds of years, and we have learned to use the principle of *ju* to preserve our pride."

Several of the smaller boys murmured agreement. Kinu looked around at the circle. "Why is it now necessary to resort to crime?"

"The White Fox says the gold will help us,"

said one of the boys, probably the youngest next to Jiro. "With money we can buy things and . . ." His voice trailed off.

"What the White Fox failed to tell you," said Zenta, "is that as soon as you start spending the money, Busuke will have proof that you were the raiders. What do you think he will do to you and your families?"

Hachiro opened his mouth to protest, but could find nothing to say. Finally he turned to Kinu. "What do you think we should do?" he asked.

"There is only one thing to do: We have to return the gold," said Kinu.

A chorus of protests came from the boys. Even Matsuzo found it hard to accept the idea of returning the gold. He had worked so hard and risked so much!

"This is stolen money," Kinu said sternly, when no one moved. "You have no right to spend it."

"You can't spend it, anyway," Zenta reminded the boys. "For a young boy to possess a piece of gold is damning evidence by itself."

"You'd better hand it to me," said Kinu. "I'll have to think of some way to return it to Busuke."

Finally Hachiro took the lead. "Here is mine," he said gruffly, walking over to Kinu and handing her his flat, oblong piece of gold. He turned to the other boys. "Our teacher is right."

The rest of the boys followed his example, some of them dragging their feet. "This is probably the last time in my life I'll ever see gold," said the youngest boy. His eyes were wistful as he handed over his shiny piece.

Watched intently by the circle of boys, Kinu placed the gold pieces on a small piece of cloth and tied the corners together. "We're still missing the pieces in the possession of your leader, the White Fox," she sighed. "But I doubt that he will have the nerve to appear."

The boys murmured angrily. "He will appear!" Hachiro insisted. "Maybe he can tell us how to spend the gold safely!"

"I doubt that very much," said Zenta. "Even your clever White Fox will find it hard to lie his way out this time."

"Lie my way out of what?" asked a voice.

13

Nobody had heard him come. Suddenly he was there, the figure in white, with the head of a fox. He stepped forward. "I thought I'd better come back, before these boys hear more slanders about me," he said.

Matsuzo peered hard at the figure. The voice sounded familiar. Was it Gombei? But if he was one of Busuke's soldiers, why would he direct the raid on the gold? Unless he was secretly planning a revolt against the occupation!

There was a tense silence, which the White Fox broke. "What didn't I tell my followers?" he asked again.

"There is the matter of the gold, for one thing," said Zenta. "Did you give each boy one piece?"

"He did!" Hachiro cried. "He shared it out as soon as we got here. There was even a piece left over we were keeping for Jiro in case he decided to join us."

Jiro looked startled and then deeply moved.

The polished wooden fox head turned toward Zenta. The change of light made its expression look reproachful. "I deal honestly with my loyal followers," said the White Fox.

Zenta looked around, counting heads. "I see seven boys here." He turned to the White Fox. "So you got the rest?"

The white figure became completely still. "One piece is for Matsuzo." The words issued from the mocking fox mouth. "I fully intended to pay him. Therefore I got one piece of gold, the same as the rest of the band."

Zenta slowly shook his head. "Not the same as the rest. That's what I meant when I said you didn't bother to tell the others everything. You're keeping back eleven pieces of gold for yourself."

"That's not true!" cried Hachiro. But it sounded more like a plea than a statement. There was some rustling from the other boys.

"You see?" the White Fox said to Zenta. "It's your word against mine, and my loyal followers prefer to believe *me*."

"I think we can find a way to check on the true amount of gold taken," said Kinu. "For instance, Gombei can tell us what the normal monthly supply is."

Unless Gombei *himself* is the White Fox! Matsuzo thought.

"You can also ask the people from the inn at the top of the hill," said Zenta. "They have no reason to lie. That was where I overheard the talk about the gold carrier."

A faint hiss came from inside the fox mask. Zenta's words had evidently come as a shock to the White Fox. This is the turning point, thought Matsuzo. At last the White Fox realized that he was in danger of losing the faith of his followers.

Hachiro moaned and looked desperately at his leader. "Tell us the truth! Tell us that Zenta is wrong!"

Matsuzo looked around at the circle of boys, and his heart ached for them. They had risked their lives to resist the conquerors. The White Fox had been their hope and inspiration. And now they had to accept the bitter truth that his motives had been completely selfish all along.

"Your greed is bad enough," Kinu said to the figure in white. "What I find most contemptible is the way you risked the lives of these boys and used them for your own gain."

The coarse kimono worn by the White Fox fluttered faintly in the breeze. It gave the impression that he was trembling, that Kinu's words had hit him hard, that her scorn hurt him more than losing the loyalty of the boys.

Then Matsuzo realized that the fluttering of the White Fox's kimono was caused by laughter.

"But I didn't plan the raid solely for gold. I did it for amusement! I was beginning to find Busuke and his men tiresome, and I wanted to do something that would seriously annoy them."

"You risked getting these boys killed because it would amuse you?" demanded Zenta.

"Did you find us tiresome, too?" cried Hachiro, his voice cracking.

The White Fox slowly looked around the clearing. Hachiro's face was twisted in anguish. The younger foxes were blinking to keep back tears. Kinu's lips were curled in contempt.

"You're right, this *is* getting quite tiresome...," he murmured. Before anyone could move, he made a sudden lunge at Kinu.

At first Matsuzo thought that White Fox was attacking her because of her scalding contempt. Then he saw that the Fox was grabbing at the bag of gold in her hand.

Before anyone could rush to her defense, Kinu acted first. Even years later, Matsuzo would remember the smooth grace of her moves. She ducked slightly, seized the left arm of her attacker, and pivoted. In a flurry of white garments, the Fox flew above Kinu's head and crashed into the ground.

For some seconds there was silence in the clearing, except for the sobbing from one of the younger boys.

Then from a distance came the metallic sound of a familiar voice. Busuke and the soldiers had finished searching the village houses, and they were now approaching the shrine.

"We'd better break up," Zenta said quickly.

"There he goes!" yelled Matsuzo. "He's escaping!"

Acting faster than anyone had expected, the White Fox had picked himself up and was already disappearing behind some trees.

Matsuzo whipped out his sword and started to run after the fugitive.

He felt his arm gripped hard. "Let him go," said Zenta. "Chasing him wastes time, and it won't help the boys."

"Why did you stop me?" Matsuzo asked angrily. "Are you going to let him get away with the rest of the gold and leave us with the blame?"

Zenta shook his head. "He won't get away with any gold. The soldiers will search him if he tries to leave the valley, so he can't afford to carry it on him."

"How can they search him?" demanded Matsuzo. "They don't know who he is!"

"But *I* do," said Zenta. "I know who the White Fox really is, and I can tell them."

Zenta's words seem to float in the air over the clearing. The boys standing around the clearing pulled back and stared.

Kinu put her arms around Jiro. "Who is it?" she whispered.

"Who is the person in the best position to hear about the arrival of the gold?" asked Zenta.

"You mean Gombei, don't you?" exclaimed Matsuzo. "He's also the one who has the best reason for getting Jiro into trouble and then rescuing him. He wants Kinu to be in debt to him!"

Kinu's face was red. "Don't be ridiculous!"

"I'm sorry," Hachiro told Kinu. "We all helped in getting Jiro framed for those thefts. But we had no idea it was Gombei."

Zenta smiled. "But it isn't Gombei! I'm talking about someone who spends time with Busuke's men at the inn, someone who overheard talk about the gold, just as I overheard."

Matsuzo began to get an inkling of what Zenta meant. There *was* someone who spent a lot of time at the inn, an entertainer who could listen to the talk of the soldiers. "You can't mean the ballad singer?" he asked, incredulously. "How can he be the White Fox? He's blind!"

"He's not blind!" Zenta said. "Furthermore, he suspects that I know he's not blind. That's why he tried to kill me."

There was a murmuring in the clearing. Zenta hadn't convinced the others, and most of the boys vehemently shook their heads. Hachiro looked angry. "I don't believe it! He couldn't have fooled us all this time!"

"The ballad singer has been coming to the valley for months!" said Kinu. "Not one of us suspected that he was only pretending to be blind. How did you find out?"

"Quite by accident," said Zenta. "The night we were running away from the soldiers, I was climbing up the hill in back with the ballad singer. It was very dark, and I had a hard time feeling my way. I noticed that the ballad singer, a blind man, was having as much trouble as I did. He even tripped over a root and fell."

"Now I see what you mean," Kinu said slowly. "In the dark, a blind man should find it easier than people with sight. He should be used to groping around without light!"

Matsuzo recalled that Zenta's voice that night had sounded strange, as if he had received a slight shock. But why hadn't Zenta told him immediately about the ballad singer's deception? Then he remembered: The two of them had been separated while escaping the soldiers. Zenta could have told him later, but he had the annoying habit of not always explaining things.

"I was surprised, of course," continued Zenta. "But I didn't see anything too sinister in it. Most ballad singers are blind; it's a standard way for them to make a living. I simply thought that here was a man who had a talent for singing ballads, and he pretended to be blind in order to be accepted into the profession."

"And then somebody pushed you off the cliff," said Matsuzo.

Zenta glanced at Hachiro, who shuffled his feet and looked uncomfortable. "That's the thing that had me so baffled at first," admitted Zenta. "Even if the ballad singer was only pretending to be blind, that alone didn't give him a motive to kill me."

Matsuzo began to understand. "But you finally understood his motive when you found out about the plan to seize the gold."

"Yes, that changed everything," Kinu said thoughtfully. "Since the ballad singer spent a lot of time at the inn, he could have heard about the gold. Therefore Busuke would naturally suspect him. But he was blind so he had to be ruled out . . ."

"Only he wasn't really blind, and he knew that you knew," finished Matsuzo. He didn't say it aloud, but he suspected that the White Fox was also jealous of Zenta. He wanted Kinu, and he saw Zenta as a possible rival.

"What are we going to do now?" asked Kinu. "Whatever it is, we'll have to hurry."

She was right. The voices of the soldiers were getting louder and closer. They would soon finish searching the shrine buildings, and they could arrive at the clearing at any moment.

"We have to arrange to return the gold," said a deep voice behind Matsuzo.

It wasn't one of the boys, and it wasn't Zenta. Matsuzo turned around and saw the shrine priest.

"You were the ballad singer's accomplice, weren't you?" Zenta asked the priest. "I should have guessed. I wondered where that beautiful wooden mask came from."

The priest nodded. "That fox mask is one of our treasures. It's hundreds of years old, and we bring it out only during certain special festivals."

"I thought the mask looked familiar!" exclaimed Kinu. "I saw it years ago as a child!"

"When the ballad singer mentioned his idea of impersonating the White Fox," said the priest, "I immediately thought of letting him use the mask."

Kinu looked at him reproachfully. "How could you do it? How could you work together with that man to corrupt our young people?"

The priest hung his head and sighed deeply. "I didn't know that he was doing the impersonation for selfish reasons. It was only now, when I overheard him admit to cheating the boys, that I finally realized what a villain he is. I thought he was doing it for the valley people, and to save our desecrated shrine."

Matsuzo remembered the broken paw of the fox statue and the slashed paintings offered by worshipers. "So you thought the money was meant for repairing the shrine?"

"He was so plausible," the priest said ruefully. "The worst part is that he was such a good singer."

"What shall we do with the gold?" Zenta asked the priest.

"I know!" said Jiro. Everyone turned to stare at him. He blushed but continued. "We can put the gold in the offering box of the shrine! The money will be used for repairing the shrine, and the soldiers can't accuse us of stealing."

The priest chuckled, and soon everyone was grinning. It was an elegant solution. The soldiers would be forced to pay for their own vandalism.

As Kinu took the bag of gold to the offering box, Zenta smiled at Jiro. "The youngest person here is the one who had the best idea."

"But the soldiers will still be furious, since half of the gold is missing," said Matsuzo. He turned to Zenta. "You said the ballad singer couldn't risk carrying his part of the loot on him. So where do you think he hid it?"

The priest broke out laughing. They all stared at him in amazement. "He didn't hide it!" gasped the priest, when he could speak again. "He asked me to keep it somewhere safe, until he could come back for it!"

There were more smiles all around. The boys had had their share of disillusionment and disappointment at having to give up their gold. But now they looked at each other with satisfaction. Since they couldn't keep the money themselves, they were delighted to learn that their false leader couldn't keep any of it, either. Even Hachiro, who usually looked glum, was smiling broadly.

"You have the gold with you?" Zenta asked the priest.

"It's in the sanctuary of the shrine," said the priest.

Even as he spoke, the unmistakable voice of Busuke sounded close at hand. He had apparently finished searching the shrine and was coming up the hill to the clearing.

"The boys mustn't be found gathered here," Zenta said quickly. "They look too much like a gang plotting something."

Since that was exactly what they had been doing, the boys didn't argue and began melting into the trees.

Hachiro smiled at Jiro and beckoned to him. Jiro's face brightened. He was accepted again. He ran to join the elder boy, and the two of them disappeared with the rest.

When Busuke's men eventually arrived, the

priest was sitting on a rock and chatting with his
visitors. He looked up at the approach of the
soldiers and his eyebrows twitched with surprise.

Busuke was in the lead, and trying to keep up
with him was a man who limped. Matsuzo tried
not to stare. The man was his recent opponent
during the raid on the gold, and he was limping
because he had a cut on his thigh—the cut from
Matsuzo's sword.

"Where are they?" demanded Busuke. His
face was red and streaked with sweat.

The priest blinked. "I don't know what you
mean."

"Don't pretend!" shouted Busuke.

The man next to him winced. He, too, was
finding Busuke's voice jarring.

"Perhaps if you will explain what you mean,"
murmured the priest, "then I can help you."

Busuke took a deep breath. With an explosion
imminent, Matsuzo put his hands over his ears.

Gombei stepped up. "I believe Busuke is
looking for the foxes who took his gold."

The man with the limp cleared his throat. "I
am Ito Tadayoshi, a retainer of Lord Yamazaki,
and I was sent here to investigate some disturbing
reports. There have been strange rumors regard-
ing foxes."

Matsuzo suppressed a groan. This man
sounded like a high-ranking samurai. He should

have known that the man was more than a mere messenger carrying gold. Then he reminded himself, *I was masked, and he can't possibly know that I am the one who fought him.*

"It's true that foxes are servants of Inari," said Zenta. "Therefore you can expect to find them here in this shrine."

"This ridiculous farce has gone on long enough!" bellowed Busuke, causing the samurai, Tadayoshi, to wince again. "We're not talking about foxes!"

"I thought that's what we *were* talking about," said Zenta.

"Let me explain," said Gombei. "Tadayoshi was carrying gold, to pay the soldiers stationed here. But he was ambushed near the mountain pass, and the gold was seized."

"He was attacked by foxes!" yelled Busuke.

"You just said you're not talking about foxes," complained Zenta.

"You also attacked *me*!" bellowed Busuke. "When I was trying to arrest that boy, you stopped me!"

Again, Tadayoshi winced at the brassy voice. His patience appeared to be wearing thin. "What happened?"

Busuke began to bluster. He seemed to realize too late that describing the affair of the futons did not add to his dignity.

"Busuke believed that the boy Jiro attacked him with a fishing pole," said Gombei. "So he and five of his stalwart men went to arrest the boy." After a moment, he added blandly, "Jiro is all of thirteen years old."

"I was hanging up some futons out in the sun, and the soldiers somehow got tangled up in them," said Kinu, keeping a perfectly straight face.

"Indeed," murmured Tadayoshi. He turned to Busuke. "Lord Yamazaki has been hearing such alarming reports about this valley that he even considered stationing additional soldiers here. When you wrote that the people were actively planning a rebellion, my lord sent me here to investigate. Now it sounds more like an affair of fishing poles, futons, and thirteen-year-old felons."

Matsuzo felt a vast relief. The investigator sent by Lord Yamazaki had come to the conclusion that nothing serious was happening.

His relief turned out to be premature.

14

Tadayoshi's eyes narrowed as he looked around. "Rumors aside, there is one thing I know for certain: The gold I carried has been stolen. I cannot rest until the bandits have been captured and the money returned."

This was the cue for the priest. His eyes opened wide, and he gasped. "Would you, by any chance, be talking about twenty gold pieces?"

"What do you know about the gold pieces?" Tadayoshi asked sharply. "And how do you know there are twenty?"

Busuke and his men pressed closer. Even Gombei stiffened. He glanced quickly at Kinu, and when she gave an almost imperceptible nod, he relaxed.

"It was the most amazing thing!" declared the priest. "I was awakened early this morning by some clinks at the offering box. I went to look into the box and caught a shining gleam at the bottom.

When I lifted the grating, I found twenty gold pieces inside!"

Moving almost as a body, the whole party went over to the offering box in front of the sanctuary building. The big box had wide wooden slats across the top, and through the slats they all saw the pile of gold pieces.

"Who put them there?" demanded Tadayoshi.

"By the time I reached the box, there was no one there," said the priest. He lowered his voice. "But I heard some high barks from a distance."

"Those are the sort of barks made by a fox," breathed one of the soldiers.

"Nonsense!" roared Busuke. "There are no foxes! It must have been those boys!"

Tadayoshi looked thoughtful. "While we were searching the houses, we found only adults, girls, and a few very young boys. What happened to the older boys?"

Kinu stepped forward. "They have gone to another valley to fish, sir. Ever since the soldiers have forbidden the boys to fish for *ayu* in our streams here, we've had to get our fish from a distance."

"That's true," said Gombei. "Busuke likes to eat *ayu,* and he doesn't want the local people to have any."

Tadayoshi stared at Busuke. "Is this true? Did you forbid the people of the valley to fish in their own streams?"

For once Busuke's voice was low. "The boys were making too much of a splash, and they were scaring the fish away."

Tadayoshi frowned. "I shall have to say something about this to my lord."

"We have to do something about the gold!" said Busuke, his voice regaining its normal volume. "We can't leave it in the offering box!" He reached for the grating and started to lift it.

"Just a moment!" said the priest. "This gold has been put here by the foxes as an offering to Inari, to atone for the desecration of the shrine."

"Nonsense!" snapped Busuke. "There are no foxes!"

"Wait," said Tadayoshi. At the tone of his voice, Busuke dropped his hands and stepped back.

"Explain," Tadayoshi said to the priest. "What do you mean by desecration?"

"You may have noticed, sir, that the paw of one of our stone foxes has been broken off," said the priest. "Some of the painted offerings have also been damaged."

Tadayoshi glanced across at the pavilion. Even at this distance, it was obvious that several of the wooden boards painted with horses had been hacked at. "What happened?" he asked.

The eyes of the soldiers went to Busuke, and Tadayoshi did not fail to notice this. "Did you and your men do this? Damage the fox statue and paintings?"

Busuke, probably for the first time since learning to talk, was at a loss for words. One of his men answered. "We had too much to drink, sir, and we got carried away."

"It's those foxes, sir," said another man. "They were always yapping at our heels! It got us really annoyed."

"This is an ancient shrine," the priest intoned solemnly. "It is dedicated to Inari, the deity of grain, and desecration of the shrine could lead to a disastrous harvest!"

There was a threat in his words. Lord Yamazaki would not be pleased if the territory he had newly conquered suffered a disastrous harvest through the fault of his own soldiers.

There was a long silence while Busuke and his men looked at their feet. "Very well," Tadayoshi said heavily. "I see that I shall have to tell my lord to send more gold."

Matsuzo was so delighted that he wanted to do a little dance. He had to make a strong effort to prevent himself from breaking out into a big smile.

But once again, his celebration was premature.

As Tadayoshi turned to leave, he suddenly stopped and turned his keen eyes on Zenta and Matsuzo. "Who are these two men?" he demanded. "They look like samurai to me. One of my attackers certainly fought like a samurai."

Gombei hesitated, and Kinu spoke first. "These men are my cousins, and they have been visiting my home for the last few days."

Tadayoshi raised his eyebrows. "You have dangerous-looking cousins."

"We are peaceful men, sir," said Zenta. "As you can see, I'm not even armed."

"You have an ugly bruise on your head," said Tadayoshi, peering at Zenta. "You must have been in a fight recently."

It's true that Zenta still looks battered, Matsuzo thought. He was also moving stiffly. "You won't believe me," said Zenta, looking embarrassed. "The fact is, I was attacked by foxes."

Someone gasped, and several of the soldiers looked over their shoulders. A whispered argument broke out.

"These men are just country bumpkins, sir, one generation removed from being peasants," said Gombei, indicating the two *ronin*. He smirked. "You have to expect a certain amount of superstition from them."

Gombei enjoyed saying that, Matsuzo thought resentfully. He let his jaw hang loose, however, and did his best to look like a country bumpkin.

Tadayoshi frowned. "Then who attacked me during the raid on the gold?" he demanded.

"I'm sure that if we had been foolhardy enough to attack you, sir," Zenta said meekly to Tadayoshi, "you would have made short work of us."

Tadayoshi opened his mouth, then closed it again.

"You must have been attacked by foxes as well, sir," said Matsuzo, with a straight face. "There are things in this valley that we are not meant to understand."

Tadayoshi stood silent, while Matsuzo held his breath. Would this formidable warrior accept the story about foxes? He would lose face if he didn't. He would have to report to Lord Yamazaki that he had lost the gold he carried to two country bumpkins and a gang of children.

Finally Tadayoshi nodded. "That's true," he murmured. "Those creatures who attacked us had something uncanny about them. I thought I was fighting quite well, and then I found myself suddenly flying through the air and landing on my back!"

Shaking his head, he turned and strode down

the stone path leading from the shrine. He couldn't quite control his limp, however.

———

Gombei and his father, Tozaemon, came to Kinu's house that evening. Gombei told them that Tadayoshi was very displeased with Busuke. "He plans to advise Lord Yamazaki to replace Busuke with someone else, someone who has a better understanding of the valley and the people here."

Zenta smiled. "I wonder whom Tadayoshi has in mind?"

The two *ronin* were eating dinner with Kinu and Jiro. It was a frugal meal of boiled millet, but it was augmented with some broiled tofu seasoned with soy sauce. This last was a luxury that Zenta had insisted on buying to celebrate the end of the crisis and the safe return of all the boys.

Kinu invited Tozaemon and Gombei to sit down and join them. "So you think Tadayoshi will ask Lord Yamazaki to appoint you as the commander of the soldiers here?" she asked Gombei.

It was Tozaemon who answered. "Of course. Lord Yamazaki's deputy has finally recognized the importance of having a local man command the soldiers here. My son is obviously the best qualified."

Gombei tried to look modest. "With Busuke gone, the locals will have less reason to resent the occupation. My job won't be too difficult."

"Busuke wasn't the only problem," observed Zenta. "You won't have the White Fox around to make trouble."

"I wonder where the ballad singer has gone?" said Matsuzo. "He was so convincing as a blind man. He had us all fooled."

"I had my doubts about him from the beginning," said Gombei. "I tried to test him several times, but he was always too alert for me."

Matsuzo suddenly remembered the time when Gombei had deliberately picked up a cup of tea meant for the ballad singer. He had probably wanted to see if the singer would automatically reach for the other cup, thus giving himself away. The test had not worked.

"The ballad singer won't have the nerve to show himself in this valley again!" said Kinu.

"Actually, I found him quite entertaining," mused Zenta. "I wouldn't mind matching wits with him again someday."

"What?" cried Matsuzo. "That scoundrel? Well, he can't pretend to be a blind man next time. Nor will he be able to borrow a fox mask again."

Tozaemon tasted the food served by Kinu and smiled at her. "Delicious tofu. You have a good touch with the seasonings, Kinu. On thinking things over, we've decided that you would be a credit to our household."

It took a moment for the implication of his last remark to sink in. A tide of red washed over Kinu's face. Jiro's mouth dropped open. He stared from Tozaemon to Gombei, and then back to his sister.

Matsuzo stole a glance at Zenta. His friend's face was completely expressionless.

Kinu knelt down on the floor, across the fire pit from Tozaemon and Gombei. The red had faded from her face, and it was now pale. "You broke off the marriage arrangements after my parents and my elder brother died," she said. Her voice was husky at first, but then steadied and strengthened. "What made you change your mind?"

Tozaemon raised his brows, looking surprised that Kinu was actually questioning him. "We thought that you were completely without family, you see."

Gombei squirmed on his straw cushion. A grimace was again distorting his mouth.

"Then what has made you change your mind?" Kinu asked Tozaemon.

Tozaemon began to look affronted. The woman he had chosen as his daughter-in-law was actually subjecting him to an inquisition. Nevertheless he condescended to answer. Indicating the two *ronin,* he said, "Now we learn that you have these cousins and are not without connections. An alliance seems desirable, after all."

He turned to Zenta. "Perhaps you will act for Kinu in restarting the marriage negotiations."

Zenta said nothing but turned to look at Kinu.

She gazed back at him for a moment and looked away. "You have been misinformed," she told Tozaemon. "These men are not my cousins. They are just sympathetic visitors, and they will be leaving quite soon."

"But . . . but . . . ," stammered Tozaemon.

Kinu's face was stony. "Therefore nothing has changed, and there is no reason to restart the marriage negotiations."

Tozaemon stared. At first he seemed to have difficulty believing he had heard right. "I see," he finally managed to say. "It seems I've made a mistake." He rose and went to the door. "We'd better leave, Gombei. We've overstayed our welcome."

After Tozaemon and Gombei had gone, nobody spoke. Finally Kinu turned to Zenta. "You *are* leaving, aren't you? I wasn't wrong about that?"

Zenta looked at her, and his eyes seemed to be pleading. "There is nothing we can do here. Your plot of land will barely support the two of you, and our supply of money will not last indefinitely. We have to go elsewhere and look for work."

"I understand," Kinu said. "Jiro and I can manage, as we have since my father died. Besides, Jiro will soon be an adult and assume his position as head of the family."

"I think you must have been managing pretty well, until the White Fox came and tried to corrupt the boys," said Zenta. There was no mistaking the admiration in his voice.

"At least you have to accept us as your cousins," Matsuzo said, trying to introduce a lighter note. "Otherwise Tadayoshi might have us arrested as vagabonds and troublemakers."

"And as cousins, we have an obligation to come back regularly to see how you are doing," said Zenta. His words were a promise.

They were quiet as they finished the rest of their meal. Then Zenta broke the silence. "I'm still puzzled about one thing," he said thoughtfully. "When we were running away from the soldiers, why did the ballad singer appear as the White Fox and distract our pursuers?"

Matsuzo thought over the question. "I guess he was hoping we would turn out to be useful— in the gold raid, for instance."

"Perhaps," said Zenta. He didn't look entirely convinced, however. "But when I told the boys that the White Fox had saved us at the bath, they looked absolutely astounded. They were masked at the time, but I'm pretty sure their reaction was total surprise."

"You're right," said Jiro. "They *were* surprised. Hachiro was telling me about that. He said that at the very moment we were running away from the soldiers, the White Fox was at Hachiro's house, outlining his plans to the gang!"

There was a long silence.

Zenta was the first to speak. "Then who was that at the bathing pool?"

Matsuzo thought back to that blurry figure they had glimpsed. It had turned around and disappeared into the woods—walking on *four legs*. He had even remarked on how convincingly the White Fox had moved like an animal.

On Kinu's face was an enigmatic smile. "Here in the valley, we are accustomed to leaving certain things unexplained."

———

The two *ronin* left the valley while it was still early morning. As they climbed, they found themselves enveloped in a swirling mist. We arrived in a fog, and we're leaving in a fog, thought Matsuzo. They were back to the beginning. He had the strange feeling that everything that had happened during the last few days had been a dream.

Fearing that he might be left behind again,

Matsuzo hurried as best as he could. To his relief he heard Zenta's voice coming out of the mist in front of him. "I thought the priest was going to keep only two pieces of gold for repairing the shrine and would return the rest. Kinu told me she was surprised he had the gall to throw all twenty pieces into the collection box."

Matsuzo stopped. "But the priest said *Kinu* was the one who threw them all in! He had put aside eighteen pieces of gold for returning to Tadayoshi, and threw only two pieces into the offering box. When he turned around, he saw all twenty pieces inside. He thought *she* had put in the rest."

They continued to climb. "I wonder who did it, then," Zenta said finally.

The fog thickened, and now Matsuzo couldn't even see Zenta's figure in front of him.

In the distance, he heard some high, yapping barks.